LOST TO THE LAKE

A gripping thriller full of suspense

ANNA WILLETT

THE BOOK FOLKS

Published by The Book Folks

London, 2022

ISBN 978-1-913516-48-2

www.thebookfolks.com

This book is dedicated to my primary school teacher who told me to stop reading books that were too grown up for me.

I didn't listen.

Chapter One

Rustling, as soft as a whisper, brought her to the surface of wakefulness. Beth turned, rolling lazily onto her side, but didn't quite wake up. With a half-smile still lingering at the corners of her mouth, she nestled into the warmth of her husband's naked back.

Marty's breathing was deep and peaceful, the only sound in the house. Its soft, repetitive rhythm soothed and beckoned her back to sleep. A moment later she woke and lifted her head from the pillow.

With her eyes half-closed, she gazed over the edge of the bed and around their bedroom. Nothing looked out of place. The room remained warm and unchanged in the glow of scented candles. The flames flickered on top of the dresser as more details of the room came into focus: the comforting aroma of citrus and vanilla, the open bedroom door, the candlelight glinting off two crystal glasses and the empty champagne bottle on the nightstand.

Still half-asleep, she thought of her dog, Angel, and wondered if Marty had forgotten to unlatch the dog door again. With mild irritation she sat at the edge of the bed, retrieved her pyjamas, then slipped them on.

She heard a sound again and realised it was the noise that had roused her, only louder this time. The rumble put her in mind of an engine running at low speed. Still drowsy, it took her a second to identify the noise. A growl. Angel never growled; he rarely barked. The thought gave her pause.

More annoyed than concerned, not with the dog but with Marty's forgetfulness, Beth padded along the hall and into the kitchen. All her husband had to do was slide back the bolt. In her mind's eye, she could see the huge dog trotting into the darkened house then snuggling into his bed in the lounge room. She smiled at the thought.

Still smiling, she thought of Marty and decided she was being unfair to him. He had more to do than worry about the dog door. Running a business was gruelling; at least that's what he kept telling her. No wonder he'd been so edgy lately. More than edgy. Marty had been touchy and as jumpy as a coiled spring. Was it any wonder he'd been so exhausted? Would it have killed her to do the little things? It's not like I have anything else to worry about, she thought wryly.

Moonlight from the window over the kitchen sink cut through the darkness and allowed her to leave the lights off as she made her way to the back door. A path she'd traversed in the dark so many times, her feet knew the way. Noting an unfamiliar but not unpleasant scent – Black Serpent aftershave perhaps – she bent to open the dog door. Angel's growls morphed into snarls; the sound so alien and ferocious that Beth jerked her hand back from the latch.

She spoke in a whisper so as not to wake Marty. "It's me. It's okay, sweetie."

Behind her, something moved. She heard the scrape of shoes on the timber flooring. A sound barely discernible over Angel's now frantic thumping at the door. Every sound she heard since first waking crashed together in her mind and formed a terrifying realisation. The rustle that woke her. Angel's growls. And now movement behind her. Someone was in the house.

Beth's heart jumped into her throat. She grabbed at the bolt desperate to let her mix-breed pit bull shepherd into the kitchen.

"Leave it."

The man's voice, aggressive and unafraid, came out of the shadows.

All the lunges, the squats, and early morning runs had done nothing to prepare her for a voice in the dark. Exercise might have strengthened her body, but not her reactions. Her legs were weak – useless. She wasn't strong or prepared to fight. A comfortable life had lulled her into complacency. How many squats would it take to make her strong enough? Her mind careened sideways with ridiculous questions. Forty squats a day over two years. How many was that?

"Why is it still moving?" the stranger asked in a relaxed, almost conversational voice.

Stupidly, Beth thought he was asking her the question and her mind worked to try and make sense of what he said.

"I threw the bait over the fence. He'll drop in a minute."

There were two of them. Two men were in her house. Her mind was working again. Men hiding in the dark; creeping out of the shadows.

"Turn around."

The harshness of the voice made her flinch.

Beth turned. Two outlines black in the moonlight.

She was a child again, huddled under the covers with fear freezing her limbs. Terrified of The Moonlight Man, a childish story her mother told to enthral Beth and her sister. *The Moonlight Man hides in the shadows because he's as crafty as the dark.* For five-year-old Beth, the Moonlight Man was a chilling spectre that dwelt in every dark corner and half-open door.

Now, twenty-seven years later, the monster had come to life. A huge shadowy figure standing before her.

"Go," the man ordered his companion.

A second shape – smaller but still threatening – stepped to the side and disappeared into the hallway. *Marty*. Her panicked mind leapt to thoughts of her husband. The man she loved, sleeping soundly, unaware of approaching danger.

"Come on," the other man said to her.

He's in charge. The realisation came quickly and out of nowhere. There were two intruders in her home. The bigger man was in control of whatever was about to happen.

As her eyes became accustomed to the gloom, she took in his imposing size – at least six feet tall with shoulders that filled the hallway. With one arm outstretched, he beckoned her closer. His other arm dangled at his side; his fist clenched around a weapon. A gun? No. Too shiny to be a gun. A glint of light bounced off the blade and Beth recognised the object as a knife.

Suddenly, her bladder felt swollen and painfully full. "What... What do you want?" she blundered out the words, her voice high and shaky.

"Let's find out." He lifted the knife and held it so the blade waved in her direction. "Come on, princess," he said.

Outside, Angel let out a low, agonised bay. When the dog's considerable weight hit the door, Beth jumped. Stumbling on numb legs, she moved towards the intruder.

Never go with your attacker. Words from a half-remembered self-defence course came to her. *The second location is always worse. Better to be stabbed* – she remembered the instructor telling the group – *than to go willingly to something far worse.* Good advice, but useless in sight of the vicious blade.

Bare feet shuffling across the kitchen, she followed the intruder's instructions. Beth heard voices. Marty's voice, loud and fearful as he asked questions, and the other man's muffled responses.

When she was close enough to smell sweat overlaid with cheap aftershave, the stranger grabbed her upper arm. His touch galvanised her and she struggled to free herself. He squeezed the flesh above her elbow then yanked her forward. Putting an end to her show of resistance, he dragged her through the hallway.

Pulled along and with her toes barely skimming the floor, Beth stumbled, grazing her knee and hitting her face on the wall. She cried out and a second later she was shoved into the brightness of the bedroom. Momentarily blinded and still off balance, she staggered and fell against the foot of the bed.

Under the glare of the lights, the horror came into jarring focus. Marty, wearing only blue boxer shorts, was sitting on the side of the bed with one shoulder slumped against the headboard. His usually carefully styled blonde hair stuck up in absurd spikes. A man in black wearing a ski mask stood over him holding a hunting knife.

"Marty!" Beth wailed. "What's happening?"

"Well, Marty here has been a very bad boy," said the man behind her, the one that was in charge. "He's taken something that doesn't belong to him. He put his hands on something he should have never touched."

"I'll give it back. Make it, make it right," Marty stuttered. "I'm sorry, okay?" He held his hands out with his palms up. "It was a mistake. I should never have... It wasn't my fault. Just don't hurt us."

"Yeah, you'll give it back. I know you'll do the right thing, but first I'm going to teach you to keep your grubby fingers to yourself," the man nearest Marty growled.

Beth, still crouched at the foot of her bed, was grabbed by the collar of her blue silk pyjamas and dragged backwards. Buttons popped and fabric ripped. Suddenly, her top gaped open leaving her exposed.

The man grabbed the tattered fabric and shook her. A second later he reached around and pressed the cold blade of his knife between her breasts.

"Now, Marty, I want you to watch and remember," he said with a touch of laughter in his voice. "I want you to see this every time you close your eyes. Every time you put those sticky fingers on your missus, remember this."

"Marty," Beth pleaded. Tears streamed down her cheeks. "Do something."

Marty shook his head. His features were set in a mask of helplessness or perhaps something else – something she couldn't quite fathom. He dropped his face into his hands. In that instance something in Beth died. It shrivelled under the feckless look on her husband's face. Their bedroom that only hours ago was their oasis now looked tawdry and ridiculous.

"Watch, asshole!" the second man, the one standing over Marty shouted.

As if to punctuate the order, he picked up the crystal glasses and flung them at the wall over the bed. They shattered and glass tumbled onto the pillows. He did the same with the champagne bottle. Each time glass hit the wall, Marty cowered and Beth sobbed.

The man holding her let go of her top and grabbed her hair. He pushed her forward and onto the bed. Behind her, she heard rustling and then the sound of a zipper being opened. Understanding struck her like a bullet. Beth pushed back and tried to get to her feet, but the man was too quick. He used his elbow to strike deep between her shoulder blades.

The air was knocked out of her lungs and she fell forward. Her mouth opened and she gasped for breath. At the same time, an explosion of glass rang out from the kitchen. For a second, no one moved.

Beth turned her face upwards and looked behind her. The man's mouth was a circle of shock. Through the eyeholes of his mask, she could see two panicked blue orbs as the sound of Angel's nails rasped and scrambled for purchase on the kitchen floor.

"Holy shit," the intruder holding the knife on Marty muttered.

Both men bolted from the room. As Beth scrambled to her feet, she heard a scream. A sound almost too high-pitched to be male.

"Angel!" Beth called and turned to run toward the kitchen.

Marty pulled her to a stop. "No," he whispered. "We need to move."

Angel bayed. The deep fierce cry echoed through the house and made the hairs on the back of Beth's neck stand on end. Something shattered and then there was more running and a shriek of agony.

"Let go," Beth hissed as she tried to shake free from Marty's grasp. "They'll kill him."

Marty wouldn't be dislodged; he dragged her towards the en-suite bathroom. "These guys don't mess around. They'll kill us both."

There was desperation in his voice and panic in his eyes. She saw the face of a man about to lose control. In that second, she couldn't say how she knew, but something told her he was ready to leave her behind. With no choice and hating herself for it, she followed him into the bathroom and slammed the door.

Marty rolled her make-up trolley in front of the door then sat on the edge of the bathtub and clenched his hands together. How, she thought, could he believe the trolley would stop their attackers?

Marty was shivering. Beth considered going to him and putting her arms around him, saying something comforting. The idea came, but just as quickly vanished.

He had let her down. He would have left her behind and saved himself. She was glad he was shivering. The thought was cruel and out of character and she immediately felt ashamed of herself. Maybe he wasn't the confident, take-charge man she thought he was, but who wouldn't be afraid when held at knifepoint? Who wouldn't panic when ambushed in the middle of the night? Still, she couldn't quite shrug off the resentment.

Pulling her tattered pyjamas closed, she wrapped her arms around her body. Her mind wanted to rerun the attack in the bedroom, but she forced herself to stay in the moment and focus on getting through whatever waited for them on the other side of the door. If only she'd thought to grab Marty's phone from the nightstand.

Straining to hear, she held her breath and listened for any sign of the men returning. Silence. The seconds ticked by. Unable to stand it any longer and tensed in readiness for the inevitable, she pushed the make-up trolley aside.

"What are you doing?" Marty asked and grabbed her wrist.

Without thinking, she shrank from his touch. His look of hurt was almost more than she could stand. He was *still* thinking of his own tender feelings even after what the intruder had tried to do to her. Or perhaps his ego was bruised because he was used to being the one in charge, she thought with distaste.

"They're gone. I'm going to find Angel," she snapped.

"You don't know that," he whispered. "They could still be out there."

Terror had drained the colour from his usually tanned face and his voice was pleading. He sounded almost child-like. How was it she'd never heard that tone before?

"What's going on, Marty?" she asked. "How do they know your name? They said you'd taken something. What were they talking about?"

"I don't know. I– I," he stuttered. "It doesn't matter. We're both okay. We just need to wait for them to leave."

"I'm not staying in here," she whispered. "Close the door behind me if you're too scared to come out."

"Beth," he called after her, but made no move to stop her as she opened the door.

The bedroom was in disarray. Glass covered the bed and the nightstand was upended. Otherwise, there was no trace of the men.

Still listening, she crept along the hallway. She had no idea what she'd do if the intruders reappeared. A vague plan of running for the front door formulated as she held her top closed against the sudden chill in the air.

A few metres further and she reached the spot where the hall met the kitchen. From where she stood, she was able to see along the T-shaped hallway that led to the front door. It stood open like a gaping black mouth allowing cold air into their home.

Certain that the men would reappear in the entrance, she ran forward and slammed the door. Fingers working frantically, she snapped the lock in place. It wasn't enough and she longed for chains and bolts – something impenetrable that would keep trespassers out.

"They must have run out the front," Marty said from behind her.

"Call the police," Beth said then headed for the kitchen.

Chapter Two

Her fingers found the light switch just as something moved in the dark. The room was illuminated, exposing the wreckage of what had taken place. A carpet of glass. A shattered vase. Blood on the floor. So much blood. Angel.

He lay on his side amidst the debris, his muscular, brindle body a mess of cuts. He was dead. Beth clamped her hands to the side of her head. Half-blind with tears, she whispered his name.

His head lifted and his amber eyes turned and sought her voice. Beth let out a whimper of disbelief and gratitude.

"Get some towels." She kept her gaze on the dog for fear if she looked away, Angel might slip into unconsciousness. "And grab my trainers," she added, too focused on the dog to care how harsh the words sounded.

Using her bare foot, she pushed aside bigger shards of glass. In response to her movement, Angel stirred.

"Stay," Beth commanded not wanting him to risk walking on the glass. "Wait."

Angel did as instructed; his eyes never leaving her face. A few seconds later Marty re-entered the kitchen. She took a towel from him and draped it across the floor then, while standing, she pulled her sneakers on one at a time.

"Okay," she said to the dog as she approached. "I'm here. You're okay now, sweetie."

With another towel in hand, she crouched beside the wounded animal and placed her palm on his head. Angel whimpered and turned to lick her fingers. Surveying his injuries, she saw a network of small cuts across his head, chest, and shoulders. Damage done when he lept through the kitchen window. On his left shoulder she noticed a deep gash.

"I need to get him to the emergency vet." She turned to Marty who was hovering in the archway. "I think he's been stabbed. Those men said something about throwing bait over the fence. He might have been poisoned too."

"Beth," Marty said. "We need to get out of here. What if they come back?"

"Stay with him while I get dressed and then call the police," she said, ignoring his response and pressing the towel to the dog's wound. "I'm taking Angel to the vet."

Back in the bedroom, she didn't waste time stripping off her torn clothes. Instead, she pulled trackpants and a loose-fitting jumper over her pyjamas. As she reached for her handbag, she noticed that her hands were shaking. Only stopping to grab a throw rug from where it had fallen off the end of the bed, she jogged back to the kitchen.

"We need to get him in the car," she said as Marty stepped aside for her.

Relieved to see that Angel was still conscious, her mind worked on how best to move him. At almost sixty kilograms it would be almost impossible to lift him without causing further injury.

The fur around his muzzle was clotted with blood. Not his blood, Beth thought with grim satisfaction. To her astonishment, Angel pulled himself into a sitting position, his mouth hanging open as he panted and watched her.

Before the dog could rise, she used another towel to sweep away the glass.

"We're going out," she said, using the familiar command to get Angel to the car.

Obedient as always, he lumbered to his feet as Beth guided him towards the hall and the door that led to the garage. He was bleeding in great dollops that left a trail on the hardwood floor. Dollops are better than drips, she thought and marvelled at Angel's resilience.

"Call the police, Marty," she said over her shoulder.

* * *

"He'll need surgery." The vet looked young, her face set in grim lines under the florescent light of the consulting room. "There's no indication of poisoning, but we'll run some blood work."

Somewhere in the depths of the building, Angel's wounds were being tended and his torn body readied for surgery.

"Will he be all right?" Beth asked as a shudder travelled up from somewhere deep inside her being. Her body was shaking. The decisiveness that had brought her this far was flagging.

The shock and trauma of the events that led up to her desperate dash to the twenty-four-hour emergency veterinary clinic had resurfaced. Intruders in her home. The physical assault. The breakneck speed she employed during the drive through mostly empty streets. It was all gaining on her.

"The wound on his shoulder is deep," the vet continued. "But the scan shows there's no damage to his heart or lungs."

The rest was lost as a flood of tears overwhelmed Beth's ability to speak or comprehend. Saving Angel's life had been the driving force in her mind and now he was safe. She was vaguely aware of the vet's questions and words of comfort.

"Go home and we'll call you when he's out of surgery." The vet gestured for Beth to be on her way. "Um, the surgery and scans are quite expensive. Six thousand dollars. We'll need half of the payment before we can commence," she continued, walking Beth towards the consulting room door.

Beth nodded, realising how it must look: Angel badly injured and her face bruised and swollen. There was no sense in hiding the truth about the break-in, but for some reason she couldn't bring herself to tell the vet what had really happened. Instead, she made up a story about Angel leaping through a window and accidently knocking her over. She included a rumour that a dog in her neighbourhood had been thrown poisoned meat. Once the lie was out, she stuck to it. Her behaviour was lunacy. On some level she understood that, but the break-in had left her feeling vulnerable, paranoid, and unsure of whom she should trust.

She was led to the reception desk where a veterinary nurse – no receptionist on duty at four o'clock in the morning – took her credit card and processed the payment. Once the bill was settled, the nurse used a button to open the entrance door. Beth walked back out into the night – a night that had begun with a celebration.

Chapter Three

There should have been police cars parked in the driveway. Could they have come and gone that quickly? Beth checked her watch and saw that more than two hours had passed since she left for the vet. She had watched enough cop dramas to know that processing a crime scene took time and that didn't include the interviews. Statements had to be taken. Why hadn't the police waited to speak to her?

She found Marty in the kitchen. Still wearing only boxers, he was cleaning blood off the floor. A two-litre bottle of bleach sat on the counter and the sting of chemicals hung in the air. When he saw her, he dumped the mop and pulled her into his arms.

"I'm sorry, pet. For everything. I just wanted us to have the world. You know I want you to have everything." He held her tight, kissing the top of her head as he spoke. "You have to forgive me. I can't do this unless you're with me."

He wasn't a bad man; he couldn't be. She couldn't be in love with a bad man. He had his faults, a temper, but that side of him was rare. She'd only seen it once or twice and thought it best not to dwell on the bad times. His temper was a small part of who he was, but tonight he'd been weak. She could live with weak, couldn't she?

She wanted him to be the man she loved. She wanted to trust him and feel the way she had only hours ago. Pressing her face against his chest, she heard his heartbeat, felt the warmth of his skin and smelled his sweat. For a few seconds she allowed herself to pretend that the horrific night had only been a bad dream. A pretence that was shattered when she opened her eyes and looked into her husband's face. He was focused on something across the room. She followed his gaze to the shape on the floor.

"What is it?" she asked, pushing free from his embrace.

Even as the question formed, she knew the answer. A body. Light blue tarpaulin, the one Marty once used to cover a hole in the roof after tiles had come loose the previous winter, now swaddled a body. Criss-crossing tape had been pulled taut around the neck. More tape turned the form into the shape of a giant bowling pin, yet the oddly moulded mass remained unmistakably human.

"He was on the other side of the kitchen bench," Marty said slowly and almost trance like. "His thigh was torn open from where Angel got him. He must have bled out."

Beth took hold of Marty's arm, not for comfort, but to steady herself as a blast of wooziness hit. Believing she was seeking emotional support, he covered her hand with his. She pulled away startled by the heat coming off his fingers.

She realised Marty was covered in perspiration. Sweat generated by physical labour. It all made horrifying sense. He found the body and inexplicably decided not to call the police. He wasn't cleaning the kitchen, but scrubbing away a crime scene and planning to do God only knew what with the dead man. Struck dumb by the insanity of the situation, she barely managed to shake her head.

"It has to be this way," Marty insisted in a rush. "If we get the police involved, it will all come out and I'll be arrested. I did some work for these guys." He pointed at the corpse. "Moved money around. I swear I didn't know they were involved in drugs."

"What?" Beth said, finding her voice. "Drugs? You're a financial planner. A mortgage broker, for God's sake. How can you be involved in drugs?"

"I'm not. I swear I'm not." He took hold of her shoulders and turned her away from the body. "But I'll look as guilty as them and I'll go to prison, Beth. I'll lose my licence as a financier." His hair, wet with sweat, clung to his face. "When they realise Angel killed that guy, they'll say he's a dangerous animal. He'll be put down."

The blows were coming fast. Marty in prison. Angel put to sleep. Beth alone. No job. No money. An image rose in her mind of the clots of blood that had coated Angel's muzzle and the satisfaction she'd felt. Knowing now that her dog had killed one of the intruders should have stirred feelings of remorse, guilt or maybe sadness. Instead, she felt only repulsed by the dead body.

The intruder was still in her house. His death felt like an ongoing assault – a vile reminder of what they had tried to do to her. She could still hear the clatter of breaking glass, only now the shards were shattering everything that felt normal and solid.

"I can't have that thing in here." She was unable to stop her voice from rising. "We've got to call someone."

She sounded petulant and spoiled. All the things she despised in others bubbled to the surface. Five years of living a privileged life had changed her.

"I know. I know." Marty held her shoulders. "You're right. We've got to get rid of him."

And just like that it had become her idea, but she wasn't the one who had broken the law. The men knew Marty, not her. This wasn't her mess.

He's taken something that doesn't belong to him. That's what the man had said while he pressed his blade between her naked breasts. Now, getting rid of the corpse was *her* idea?

"I've packed a bag," he continued. The old Marty was back and taking control of the situation. Part of her was relieved because if he took control, she would be able to shrink from it. She could distance herself from what was happening. "You go and throw a few things in a suitcase."

He went on and on planning every step. "I used the spare tarp still in the packet so there's no prints. We'll drive down south. Spend a few days somewhere. We always enjoy a few nights away. Yes, something we often do," he said more to himself than to her. "We'll find a spot – a national park. If we go off the beaten track, they won't find him for years, if ever."

"Are you insane?" Beth snapped. "We can't dump a body. We're not those people." She searched for the right words. "We're not criminals."

Marty let her go and returned to mopping. As his shoulders worked, the scar on his back bulged and rippled. The old burn mark was large and knotted with mottled skin. The scar was from a childhood fall onto a hot barbeque. She had always loved him even more because of it. She loved his imperfections and ached for the pain he must have endured. How many times had she traced that scar with her fingers? A thousand times at least, but even the most familiar part of him now looked alien.

"It'll work. Trust me. I can use the cardboard from the box the new fridge came in. It's still in the garage." Now he was definitely talking to himself. "With a bit of duct tape, it'll do to cover the broken window. It shouldn't have shattered like that, but if it was cracked, who knows? I'll get someone out when we get back."

The man furiously mopping was a new Marty, one that Beth barely recognised. His cheeks were streaked with perspiration. His hair was damp and matted over his forehead. He was a man poles apart from the affable, latte-drinking financial adviser that she had fallen in love with. But more than anything, it was the look in his eyes that worried her. A frantic look of searching and plotting that she couldn't begin to gauge.

Exhausted and too wrung out to argue, she returned to the bedroom and began packing. Carelessly, she opened drawers and stuffed clothing into a suitcase. The spot between her shoulders was a throbbing reminder of the moment the intruder had forced her to her knees. While she packed, she kept her eyes averted from the bed and its blanket of shattered glass.

She continued this way for ten minutes before she realised her hands were still stained with blood. Angel's blood. Horrified, she rushed into the bathroom and scrubbed her palms and fingers under hot water.

Watching the water turn from brownish red to clear, she felt reason and normality running away. Caution and scruples were trickling down the drain with the blood-tinted water, leaving only the need to escape the gore and violence. The need to put the night of broken glass behind her. Maybe then she could be Beth again. Normal Beth.

Chapter Four

Marty reversed Beth's car out of the garage and backed in his car. His Mazda had more boot space and was perfect for travelling. Only this time they stored their luggage and coats on the back seat.

"Once we get him in the boot," Marty said, now showered and dressed in a pair of faded jeans and an old jumper that he usually wore when cleaning out the gutters, "we can put the other stuff on top of him."

He spoke with the casualness of a man preparing for a fishing trip or a jaunt into wine country. *Put the other stuff on top of him.* Spade, bleach, gloves, water bottles, torches, and a bag of clothes to change into after they were done burying the corpse. Just *stuff.*

The sun was coming up. Its pallid rays snaked their way around the gaps in the now boarded-up window and shone on the tarpaulin. Seeing the body in daylight, even in weak daylight, made the horror of what they were about to do seem undeniably real.

"You take the legs," Marty said.

Say no, she thought. Bring the madness to an end. She longed to be anywhere but inside the gloomy kitchen, still wearing tattered pyjamas under her clothes. She wanted to be somewhere far away from the stench of bleach and blood that burned her nostrils.

It was all so wrong. Some juvenile, stupid part of her clung to the belief that it would all be over when the sun came up. A new day would wipe away the night-time horrors. Wasn't that how it was supposed to work? But those tiny reeds of sunlight didn't cleanse; they exposed. It would never be over. What they were about to do would lock them into a nightmare – one they were doomed to share forever. Like a secret kiss. A black, ugly embrace from which there would be no escape.

Her phone was on the counter. Why not call the police? Why not put an end to Marty's temporary insanity? That's what it was. It had to be. He would see reason once the cops arrived and maybe he wouldn't thank her, but at least he would feel release for laying down this hellish burden.

Police, prison, alone. The words kept dancing in her mind. Marty taken away. Angel put to sleep. Her alone. No money. No home. If she picked up the mobile, what would Marty do? Above all else, the fear of Marty's unpredictable reaction gave her pause.

As if answering her thoughts, her phone rang. Beth jumped. Marty let out a startled whoop then clamped a hand over his mouth. In that moment he really did look unhinged.

Seconds passed as they listened to the mobile ring. Finally unable to stand the harsh trill any longer, Beth snatched up the phone. It would be the police. She accepted the inevitable with flat certainty. It didn't matter how they knew, just that it was over.

"Mrs Jacobsen?"

Beth didn't recognise the woman's voice, but why would she? The formal greeting could only come from a police officer, and in a way Beth was grateful.

"Yes." Beth managed to get the word out with some semblance of certainty.

"Angel is doing well. He's awake and has been outside for a wee."

"Angel," Beth repeated. Not the police, but the vet. "He's okay?"

"Oh, yes," the woman continued. "He came through like a champ. We had to give him blood, so we'll keep him in tonight and all going well, if he eats, drinks, and wees again, he can go home tomorrow. Dogs usually recover faster in familiar surroundings."

Relief felt like a summer downpour, a warm rain that washed away the tension and cleared the air. Angel was okay. Beth could cope with what they were about to do as long as she had Angel to come home to.

"We're sending you a snap of him. He's a very gentle boy." Beth could hear a smile in the vet's voice. "I can see how he earned his name. He's been so good, letting us do whatever without complaint," she continued. "But best not to visit because he'll think he's coming home. We will let you know as soon as he gets the all-clear."

Beth turned her back on Marty and the dead body. "I can't thank you enough. I'm glad he's being good. He is a very special dog." She stopped as emotion made her throat constrict.

"Yes, he's a dream. Now, we'll keep you in the loop," the vet said before hanging up.

"Okay, that's good," Marty said when she told him the news.

But with his eyes jumping between her and the body she doubted he'd taken in much. She wanted to be annoyed, but couldn't summon the strength. Could she blame him for being distracted when their lives and freedom depended on what they were about to do?

He gestured to the body. "We need to do this now, Beth."

* * *

When she was twelve, she found her guinea pig Mr Sprinkles unmoving in his cage. Thinking he was asleep but at the same time concerned because she'd never actually seen Mr Sprinkles lie down to snooze, she reached in and picked him up.

At twelve she knew very little about death, but even to her childish hand the feel of something dead was unmistakable. Soft yet hard and unnaturally heavy; Mr Sprinkle's body resisted her touch.

The dead legs had that same feel, even through the latex gloves that Marty insisted they wear. The body had a dirty secret quality, like something that wasn't meant to be touched, not by living hands. Grunting, Marty shuffled backwards as they turned the body in a circle then headed for the garage entrance, off to the side of the main living room.

It was heavy. Beth decided it would be easier if she thought of the corpse as 'it' and not 'he'. He who had held a knife to her husband and had urged Marty to watch as the other man assaulted her. The other man. She hadn't considered how he would figure in what they were doing.

"What about the other guy?" she asked through gritting teeth. "The bigger one. He knows what happened. What if he tells someone or something?" What if he comes back? *Comes back*. The thought made her hands jittery. So much so that she almost let go of its ankles.

"Don't drop it," Marty hissed. "Let's get it in the boot and then we can worry about the rest."

The rest? Was there more to come? More midnight visits from the man in the ski mask?

* * *

Quentin wheeled his bike toward the road, lime-green safety helmet clamped snugly on his head. As Marty reversed out of the garage, Quentin raised his hand in a neighbourly greeting. Beth waved back hoping their neighbour would climb on his ridiculous racing bike and make tracks.

Not to be put off, Quentin smiled and turned the bike's front wheel in their direction then used his foot to hit the kickstand down. Clearly, he was hoping for an early morning chat.

"Jesus," Marty muttered under his breath then lowered his window.

Beth had never warmed to their neighbours. Quentin's plummy voice always struck her as an affectation. He was a man who believed himself to be superior to those around him. And all the frantic urban cycling seemed tragically desperate for a man approaching fifty. Quentin appeared to be trying to beat the aging process by speeding through the streets at the crack of dawn.

But was she any better? Gym memberships, facials, manicures, and waxing. Beth was just as frantic in her own attempts to reach perfection. And why was she only now realising that there was something dreadfully lonely in her empty existence? Almost as tragic as a middle-aged man in green lycra?

"You're off early," Quentin said, making the observation sound more like a question.

Head turned away, so their neighbour wouldn't see the swelling on her cheek, Beth rummaged through her handbag. Her peak cap was on the back seat somewhere beneath the bags. Why hadn't she thought to put it on?

"Heading down south," Marty replied. "Better to hit the road early and miss peak hour."

"What peak? It's Sunday." Quentin turned to look at the almost empty street as if for confirmation.

"Yeah, but that's when everyone's hitting the road," Marty said.

"Too true. Good idea." Quentin's voice was starting to grate on Beth's nerves. "It's a plan."

She found her sunglasses and slipped them on, hoping they would cover enough of her face so as to obscure the obvious signs of injury. What, she wondered, would their fitness enthusiast neighbour think if Marty told him they had a corpse in the boot? *Yeah, good idea.* That seemed to be the man's go-to answer.

"Lorraine and I thought we heard glass smashing last night," Quentin continued, balancing one foot on the kickstand. "Did you hear anything?"

"Yeah, sorry about that, but the dog got spooked and jumped through the kitchen window," Marty responded without missing a beat. "He gave us a scare. Didn't he, pet?"

It took Beth a second to realise Marty was talking to her.

She let her long, dark hair fall over her face as she glanced toward the open window. Quentin was leaning closer, wide eyes and peering in her direction. It looked like he was waiting for her to speak.

"Yes." She managed a nod. "Scary."

"Christ." Quentin looked aghast. His chin strap bunched the skin around his neck in a way that made him look like he was being strangled. "Is he okay?"

"Oh, yeah. Yeah, he's fine," Marty jumped in. "Just a few scratches."

Up until that moment Beth had thought of nothing but the contents of their boot and how Quentin was standing within a metre and a half of a dead body. But listening to the smooth, unworried quality of Marty's voice as he described Angel's injuries, his dismissiveness made her want to lash out. Not with her hands, although they were curling into fists, but with her tongue.

She wanted to scream something hurtful or embarrassing. Call him a lying bag of pig shit because he *was* a liar. A smooth liar. He certainly kept her in the dark about what really went on at his office. Marty did a neat job of hiding how he made his money.

"Yep, will do," Marty said to wrap up the conversation.

Beth had missed whatever else Quentin had to say about the smashed window and her injured dog.

"Have a good one, buddy," Marty said, putting the window up.

It wasn't until they were turning out of their street that she managed to uncurl her fists.

Chapter Five

The freeway always unnerved her. Travelling in narrow lanes – vehicles skimming by only centimetres from a collision – while racing at breakneck speed, filled her with anxiety. The danger seemed almost palpable. A siren wailed behind them and Beth hissed out a curse.

"Take it easy," Marty said, checking the mirrors.

She wanted to shriek, hurl accusations and berate him for putting her in this situation and getting her involved in something that would no doubt lead to their arrests. The siren grew louder as it closed in on them. Would this be the moment when it all came crashing down?

Would the police make her lie on the road the way she'd seen them do in films with criminals? A lump formed in her throat and no matter how hard she tried, Beth couldn't swallow. She couldn't generate a drop of moisture in her mouth. Marty pulled left, seemingly ready to accept the inevitable. Her fingers were coiled around the door handle as the ambulance barrelled past and the shrieking of its siren engulfed the car.

"Must be an accident," Marty said with mild curiosity.

Peeling her hand off the door, she didn't trust herself to respond. Marty pulled back into the flow of cars and within seconds they were hurtling forward.

When her heart finally returned to a steady beat, she asked, "Where are we going?"

"While you were packing, I booked us three nights at a place called White Mist Lake Retreat. It looks nice," he replied, sounding genuinely enthusiastic. "It will be good for us to take a few days off after – you know – we do what we have to." He tilted his head toward the rear of the car.

"We can spend some time together," he continued. "Just soak up the peace and quiet. Go hiking. Talk. Like couples therapy."

"Couples therapy." She repeated the words incredulously.

"Yeah," he said. "We need this. And I promise it will bring us closer. We'll come back stronger. It's what you always said you wanted."

At a loss and not sure she could believe what she'd heard, Beth rubbed her forehead. "But when I said couples therapy, I meant we'd go and see someone together. Talk through our issues."

"This will be better. Trust me," Marty replied.

She could almost feel his desperation, but the last thing she wanted was to sit in a cabin thinking about how their lives had been demolished. And their relationship? Every time she caught herself wanting to fall into Marty's arms and let him tell her everything was going to be okay, the memory of his resigned expression flooded her thoughts. The image of the way he dropped his face into his hands while the intruder stuck the knife between her breasts surfaced like an ugly monster.

"I can't spend three nights at some retreat," she said. "I have to pick Angel up tomorrow."

"Yes, I thought about that. You can ring the vet and ask them to board him for a few nights. It'll probably be better for him to stay where he's getting such great care. Better for Angel's recovery."

"How are you doing this?" she asked, unable to keep the astonishment out of her voice.

"Doing what?" He glanced her way with a glimmer of something dark in his eyes.

"Planning all this?" Beth circled her arm in the air. "Being so calm?"

"What do you want me to do, Beth? Fall apart?" The sudden anger in his voice made her flinch. "Is that what you want? Because you know we'll both be in the shit if that happens."

She had never seen him like this – so quick to erupt. Well, almost never. After five years together, four as husband and wife, she realised she was getting a crash course on Martin Jacobsen. Nothing like a home invasion, assault, and death to bring a couple together.

"No, I don't want you to fall apart," she said calmly. She wanted him to watch the road as the speedometer ticked up to one hundred kilometres per hour. "We just need to talk. I need to know what's going on because everything is moving too fast and I feel like I can't breathe."

He let out a long sigh and his shoulders slumped. "I'm doing the best I can to get us out of this mess. Can you just trust that? Cut me some slack and, and…"

For the first time since she returned home to find him with the body, Marty seemed distressed.

He was right, she realised. He *was* doing his best. Right or wrong, at least he was thinking. If it'd been up to her, Marty would be in police custody by now. Or, they would both still be standing over the corpse wringing their hands.

"I know." She put her hand on his arm. "I know you're trying to sort this out, but we need to pull over somewhere and talk through the plan." When he didn't answer, she tried again. "I can't help if I don't know what we're doing. I *need* to know, Marty."

The resentment and disappointment she'd been nursing for the last four hours hadn't quite dried up, but at least it was cooling off. It had settled into something that she could put away, for now. Marty was scared and tired. As tired as her. She could see that now.

Seeing him slumped and bewildered made her think of what happened in their bedroom, only this time she asked herself the all-important question. What had she expected of him? Had she wanted him to take on two armed men like an action hero? She didn't have to think about the answer because it was an easy yes.

Marty was tall; a fit guy who spent hours at the gym. He had a temper – one she'd seen up close. So yes, she most definitely expected something more than that heartbreaking look of resignation on his face. A look that said, 'What are you gonna do? Rape and humiliate my wife, but make it quick.'

She stopped herself – stopped the avalanche of bitterness. He was only human – just a man faced with two armed intruders. They were alive. If Marty had tried something stupid, they might both be as dead as the man in the boot.

She noticed his features wrestle into some semblance of calm. He was holding it together, not by much, but at least he was trying; trying to get through the ordeal and make things right again. Seeing him struggling made the resentment she'd been carrying seem too heavy a burden. It was a cruel and selfish barrier that had allowed her to take the moral high ground.

"It will be over soon," she said. "You've got a plan. A good one, I'm sure. It'll work and then we can go back to normal."

The little speech sounded convincing, not that she really believed what she'd said. All that mattered was the look of gratitude on Marty's face. All she wanted was to wake up from the nightmare and find herself at home in their safe little house.

"What he tried to do to you… It eats me up. I should have—"

"It's over now." She took hold of his shoulder and squeezed. "We'll be okay."

He nodded then took her hand and kissed it. She felt a fierce need to protect him, to protect them. It soothed some of the bitterness.

"You need coffee," she continued. "And something to eat. We both do."

"Okay." He still seemed a bit dazed, but calmer. "We'll get something at the drive-thru. The big food and fuel hub – the one just before the Forrest Highway."

"Is it safe?" she asked. "The cameras and everything?"

"Yes, it's normal for us to stop for food on the way." The enthusiasm was back in his voice. "It's perfect, big, always busy. We'll fill up the tank as well. Use the bathroom."

* * *

Fifteen minutes later, they pulled in to the refuelling station. Marty was right about it being busy. The bustling hub and the rush of people turned every face into that of an anonymous traveller. Watching him pump petrol, knowing they were on camera for all the world to see, made Beth squirm with anxiety. She imagined sitting in court viewing a black-and-white video tape. Security footage on TV always looked grainy and black and white; the lack of colour giving the suspects a criminal look.

Martin Jacobsen can be seen using the fuel pump while his wife waits calmly in the car. In her mind, she could hear the prosecutor's voice echoing in the courtroom. *The footage speaks for itself. The Jacobsens were in no hurry. What this film shows is a cold-blooded disregard for human life.*

Despite the chilly July air, beads of sweat popped out on Beth's underarms and trickled down her sides. Someone yelled and she swung around in her seat expecting to see cops approaching the rear of the vehicle.

Instead, a girl in an oversized fleecy jumper – there was a name for those blanket-like ponchos, but Beth couldn't think of it – and Ugg boots was slapping a young guy on the shoulder with her head thrown back in laughter and a jumbo-size soft drink in her other hand.

When Marty opened the door and sat back in the car, she felt her muscles relax slightly. They were almost done. A crowd was good. It was easier to be overlooked in a crowd, but at the same time there were too many people and too many eyes on them.

"Okay," he said, starting the car. "I'll pull around the side and we can use the bathroom."

Beth needed the toilet. Until Marty mentioned it, she had been clenching her gut, trying to ignore the pressure. But now she realised she had to go.

"We can't both go at the same time," she said when he parked. "We can't leave the car."

"It's fine," Marty said, sliding out from behind the wheel. "I'll lock it."

He was right, of course, yet leaving the vehicle unattended seemed wrong – careless. Anything could happen. A fire. An explosion. A fender bender. She could see it clearly in her mind's eye. The two young kids that were laughing a few minutes ago pulling out of the hub. The girl wearing the Oodie – the word Beth had been searching for finally came to her – driving and sipping her over-sized fizzy drink, clipping their car on the way out. Nothing major. Just the rear end. A ding that dented the bumper and smashed open the boot.

"I'll wait until you come back," she called from the passenger seat.

Marty shrugged and sauntered toward the toilet block with the maddening ease of someone that had all the time in the world. Not for the first time that day she wondered how much she didn't know about her husband.

* * *

Above the sprawling hub, a sign offered an assortment of fast-food options: fried chicken, burgers, meat pies or sandwiches. They settled on the burger place and pulled up to the drive-thru window. With the car smelling of fried eggs and coffee, they headed for the highway.

A few kilometres further, Marty pulled off the road and into a neglected-looking rest stop where a dented sign that sat amidst calf-deep weeds warned drivers about the dangers of fatigue. Wearing their winter coats, they occupied one of two picnic tables.

The cold breeze brushed Beth's cheeks as she turned her face up to the sun. For a moment, the rumble of trucks and the swish of speeding cars faded away. It seemed like an age since she'd last experienced a few seconds of peace.

"Drink up," Marty urged, setting the cups and brown paper bag on the table.

Beth drank the coffee in gulps. The lukewarm liquid tasted strong and creamy. Her stomach reacted to the bag's greasy smell, with groaning hunger. By the time she unwrapped her bacon and egg muffin, Marty had already finished eating.

"We'll keep an eye out for side roads, national parks or anything that looks old or unused. We're looking for a spot that isn't likely to attract tourists. Then we'll check into the cabin," he said, wiping his mouth with a napkin. "We can grab some maps. They always have maps at bush retreats. We wash up, get some sleep, and then go out when it's dark."

She was struck by his ability to plan. How, she wondered, was he able to block out the guilt and focus so clearly? She didn't know whether to be grateful or nervous.

"And what about the other guy?" she asked around a mouthful of food. "You said they'd come back. He knows what Angel did to his partner. All the more reason to come looking for us."

Marty's features were motionless, his eyes hidden behind sunglasses. Still, she thought she saw a tick of irritation.

"One," he began, "he doesn't know where we are and, two, he's not as likely to risk doing anything on his own." He balled up the napkin. "We're okay for now. Concentrate on that."

Beth thought for a second. "How do you know *what* he'll do? He said you took something that didn't belong to you. Was he talking about money? Are you going to give it back?"

"Listen," – Marty stood and looked around for a rubbish bin – "I'll sort it all out after we've taken care of... *you know*. You wanted to know the plan. Now you do." His voice softened. "The best thing we can do is focus on today."

It wasn't even close to an answer. In fact, he had been deliberately avoiding her questions all morning and the constant uncertainty was starting to wear her down. She knew Marty had a talent for being evasive, but usually he did it with more charm.

"Damn it, Marty—" She stopped when she spotted an ancient-looking white station wagon pulling in behind their Mazda.

"We should go," Marty said, watching as an elderly man climbed out of the old car and pressed his hands to the small of his back.

Quickly dumping their rubbish in the overflowing bin, Marty took hold of Beth's arm and steered her towards the vehicle.

"Nice ride," the man said when they drew closer. "You don't happen to have a spare bottle of water, do you?"

Beth had one hand on the car door, but hesitated, not sure what to do. They had water. They had plenty of water in the boot. For one crazy moment she thought Marty might oblige the man and open the boot.

"Sorry, mate," Marty replied. "Only the ones we're drinking out of."

"I've got a cup." The elderly man was neatly dressed in dark pants and a grey hoodie. "Just a few sips. I'm parched."

Marty hooked his hands on his hips. Beth recognised the stance; he was thinking. She looked from her husband to the older man who looked to be somewhere north of sixty. While Marty contemplated the stranger, the seconds ticked by in uncomfortable silence.

"Yeah, no worries," Marty finally replied cheerfully. "You've gotta stay hydrated even in this weather."

Marty had charm – natural charm – and an easy smile that dimpled his cheeks. There was an implied good humour in his tone paired with just the right amount of okka. This wasn't the first time Beth had seen Marty's charisma at work, but it was only now that she was able to watch the spectacle with a detached eye – detached enough to break down his voice and body language. If not for the dead body in the boot, she probably would have been entranced by Marty's good-guy routine.

Instead, Beth turned her attention to the older man and watched as he dove into the back of his station wagon while Marty opened the driver's door. The windows of the station wagon were grimy. Beth noticed a sleeping bag and a couple of bulging, oversized laundry bags. Was the guy homeless or on a camping trip?

A minute ago, she saw the stranger pull in behind them, his car heading in the same direction as theirs. That meant he would have passed the fuel hub less than ten minutes ago. Why didn't he get water there? If he didn't have any money, there was always the taps in the toilet block.

Marty pulled a metallic water bottle out of the console then came and stood next to her. As they watched the stranger rummage through his belongings, the two of them exchanged looks. Both wearing dark glasses, it was little more than an acknowledgement of the oddness of the situation. Beth gave a slight nod toward the road, indicating that they should go.

"Yep, knew it was here." The stranger produced a blue, plastic cup that he held out for Marty to fill. "My name's Rod, by the way."

As he moved closer, Beth caught a whiff of body odour and unwashed hair and resisted the urge to shudder. When Rod lifted the cup to his mouth, his lips pulled back, revealing brownish black teeth.

"You're a lifesaver." The older man slurped the water like a man dying of thirst. "Sorry. What did you say your names are?"

A bad feeling slithered into the pit of her stomach. It could have been the greasy muffin, but Beth suspected it had more to do with the sly, covetous glint in Rod's rheumy eyes – eyes that crawled over Marty's face, hair, and clothes.

"I'm Keith and this is Nicole," Marty said without missing a beat as he screwed the lid back on the water bottle.

"Could you lend me five bucks, Keith?" Rod shuffled closer. "See? I've lost my ATM card and I need fuel to get me home."

Not waiting for an answer, Rod turned his attention to Beth. "That's a nasty bruise, Nicole. Turning into a real shiner. You should put some ice on it."

"Sorry, mate," Marty said, ignoring the man's comment about Beth's cheek. "I don't carry cash. But have a good one—"

Before Marty could finish, a phone rang, not Marty's or Beth's chirping bell, but a snatch of rap music. Beth looked at Rod expecting him to go for his pocket. He surprised her by shrugging and glancing at the Mazda.

"Your phone's ringing," Rod said, nodding toward the boot.

The food in Beth's gut roiled. Marty had forgotten to empty the dead man's pockets before wrapping him in the tarp. Another thought occurred. Did Rod know? Was he somehow connected to the men that had broken into their house? Needing water seemed a lame excuse for approaching them. Perhaps the older man had followed them from the city. When they left home, why hadn't they thought to check and see if anyone had been watching the house? They'd been careless – careless enough to get them killed.

"Yep," Marty replied. "There it goes again."

Incredulous, she turned to look at her husband. His voice and appearance seemed relaxed. She started to wonder how he could be so calm when she noticed that Marty wasn't calm at all. There was a tenseness to his features and his hands had returned to his hips. Marty was thinking again.

The fingers on Marty's right hand were ticking. Not drumming, but sort of flicking in and out. A crazy image popped into her mind of a gunslinger in an old Western. She wished she knew what he was contemplating because there was something ominous in the way he was watching the older man.

"Aren't you going to answer it?" Rod asked.

For the first time since approaching them, the older man seemed unsure of himself. He looked from Beth to Marty then gave a nervous laugh.

"No," Marty replied. "I know who it is." His charm had evaporated as a hard edge crept into his tone.

What was he thinking? This new husband of hers, the one who knew how to dispose of dead bodies and always had a plan, was almost unreadable. Beth put her hand on the crook of his arm and applied pressure – backwards pressure. *Let's go* pressure.

"Funny place to keep your phone," Rod said. To Beth's relief, he jammed his fist in his pocket and fished out keys while turning toward the station wagon.

Marty refused to budge so Beth gave up on trying to pull him away. Not sure what to do next, she remained next to Marty and watched as Rod climbed into his vehicle while muted rap music drummed out from inside the boot.

"You have a good one, buddy," Marty called as Rod slammed his car door.

A moment later, the station wagon's engine roared, faltered, then caught. Beth and Marty remained in place watching until the car joined the anonymous stream of traffic.

Chapter Six

Beth laced her hands through her hair. "This is getting crazy."

They were back on the highway and heading south. Above them, the sun hung partially hidden by clouds that cast claw-like grey shadows on the road.

"I don't think I can do this, Marty. He heard the phone. Don't you see?"

Marty kept his gaze on the road. She was grateful for that because they were flying along. Trees and properties were whizzing by at a sickening speed.

"Slow down," Beth cried. "If we get pulled over or have an accident..."

"Yeah, I hear you," Marty replied and eased up on the accelerator. "I'll fix this, Beth."

A turning came up. Marty veered left and exited the highway. Beth wasn't quick enough to catch the name of the road, but saw a sign warning of heavy vehicles, indicating that the road led to a quarry or an industrial area.

Minutes later, they turned onto a tightly packed dirt track. Dense bush crowded both sides of the Mazda. Usually as dry as kindling in summer, the undergrowth now flourished lush, green and dense under the winter rain.

Marty killed the engine and sat motionless. Beth unbuckled her seat belt and turned to scan the track for cars.

"That man, Rod. He could be following us," she said.

"Forget about him," Marty replied. "He's just a yobbo. Probably hangs around bothering tourists for money all the time."

"But he heard the phone," Beth persisted. "You left the phone in the guy's pocket. Didn't you think to look before wrapping him up? Didn't you check his pockets?"

Without warning, Marty struck the steering wheel with the ball of his hand. "Fuck!" He continued pounding the wheel while gritting his teeth and repeating the obscenity over and over.

Beth had never seen him like this, so enraged, so out of control. She had no idea what to say or how to calm him. That's not true, she reminded herself. She *had* seen this before. Without realising she was doing it; she pressed her back against the passenger door to widen the space between them.

"Marty, stop. I'm sorry. You'll hurt yourself."

The sudden explosion of rage dissolved with unnerving speed. Marty's hand dropped into his lap. He was breathing heavily and still not looking at her. As frightened as she was of their situation and his violent outburst, she could see that Marty was on a wire – a thin line between control and despair. If she didn't step up, that wire might snap.

"All you have to do," she began while trying to sound calmer than she felt, "is get the phone and take the battery out. We can smash it and then bury it or dump it somewhere."

She wasn't sure if he was listening until he gave a nod.

"Right," he said. He was coming alive before her eyes. "The battery and the sim card."

Without saying another word, he leapt out of the car. Beth got out and followed him to the back of the vehicle, grateful that the storm seemed to have passed.

Seeing the swaddled corpse again jolted her back in time: the blade cold against her skin, broken glass glinting on their bed. She couldn't bear to see what was under the tarp. Feeling like a coward, she turned and walked along the trail until it reached a slight incline.

"I'll watch for cars," she called over her shoulder, not sure if he could hear her.

The breeze kicked up, lifting her hair and making her shiver. She wished she had grabbed her coat. A quick glance over her shoulder and she saw Marty leaning into the boot. *He's taking too long.* Painfully aware of how exposed they were, she wanted it to be over. Even the idea of speeding along the highway was preferable to having the boot open with the risk of someone driving over the rise and seeing the corpse.

The wind carried the sound of ripping tape and the crackle of plastic. Beth kept her eyes on the track while a crow cawed an accusing cry from a nearby tree. Or was it a caw of hunger? Scavengers could smell death. Had the body already attracted attention?

Another few minutes – although it seemed longer – and the boot slammed. Beth let out a shaky breath then plodded back to the car.

Marty held a phone in one gloved hand and a wallet in the other. He clamped the wallet under his arm and then he turned the mobile over and fiddled with the back casing. As if awakened by his touch, the phone rang again. After an age of thumping rap music and fumbling, he pulled the battery free and the mobile fell silent.

"Here." He pulled a blue latex glove out of his front pocket and handed it to her. "Put this on and hold the wallet."

Beth obeyed silently and watched as Marty found a rock and went to work on the battery.

"Wait here," he said seemingly to himself. "I'm going to bury these and we'll ditch the phone and wallet somewhere else."

It took only seconds for him to disappear into the thick brush. Beth turned the wallet over and flipped it open. A couple of fifty-dollar notes were in a side flap and there was a driver's licence behind the plastic window. Lenton Hubbard. Neither the name nor the photo meant anything to her. When she'd seen him alive, Hubbard had been wearing a ski mask and brandishing a knife. It wasn't surprising that she didn't recognise his photo.

Still, seeing his name and face made him seem more real, no longer just a masked stranger. He was a human being, a man with a name and perhaps a family. Now he was dead and in the back of their car.

Yesterday, she'd been giddy with excitement as they celebrated what Marty described as a 'big client'. They drank champagne, made love, and planned a trip to Fiji. Those carefree hours seemed like a faraway memory. The seemingly happy couple had now become two different people.

When Marty's hand touched her shoulder, she gasped.

"Done," he said, pulling her closer. "Sorry I freaked out before." He spoke into her hair so she couldn't see his face.

"No," she replied. "*I'm* sorry. I know how hard you're trying. I didn't mean to sound like I was blaming you."

She pulled back and lifted his sunglasses then pushed them to rest on his hair. His hazel eyes were red-rimmed and tired, but they were still the same smoky shade. Five years ago, she found herself infatuated by the glint of mischief in those eyes. Now she couldn't be sure if that feeling was still alive. He kissed her. The light touch of his lips was so cool and passionless that it left her more confused than ever.

"We should get out of here," he whispered.

Chapter Seven

Five years earlier

It wasn't a date, just coffee; yet she took her time selecting an outfit. Settling on a yellow blouse and black jeans – tight jeans – together with high-heeled boots to accentuate her already long legs, Beth used swift, expert strokes to blow-dry her hair. Finally, she added a touch of mascara to her dark lashes.

She reminded herself that everything was still okay. She hadn't lied. That was the important thing. Not mentioning something wasn't the same as lying. Besides, nothing had happened outside of a bit of harmless flirting. And why not? Work had been tough lately and she deserved a distraction. Later, she would come home happy and make love to Ethan.

It was a win-win, really. She would enjoy a safe little ego boost and Ethan would be treated to spectacular sex. What difference did it make where she got the inspiration as long as the act took place at home? She could hardly believe forming sexual fantasies involving one of her clients was already on her mind.

She had only cut the man's hair three times and the last two times had been unnecessary. They both knew he wasn't there for a haircut. It was sort of sweet, really, she thought once she was behind the wheel with her eyes peeled for a side street. The last time she saw Martin – she didn't know his last name – he had trouble meeting her eyes in the mirror. A good-looking guy like him too shy to look at *her*.

She parked well away from the café and made sure the old rattler she drove was out of sight. The last time Martin was at the salon, he had parked out front and she had watched through the window as he eased his athletic body out of a sporty little Alfa Romeo. Not that she cared what he thought of her, only her Suzuki was more than ten years old and with the ding in the driver's door it looked ready for the scrapyard.

It would probably be the last time she did anything remotely wild. It was silly, really, to get so excited over a coffee. Did that say something about her life? She had been living with Ethan for two years – two good years. Both his sisters were married. One had a two-year old. Beth knew Ethan's mother was waiting for them to announce their engagement *or* a pregnancy. Ethan wanted both and so did Beth, sort of.

But it was all so mapped out. The word stifling came to mind and she quickly dismissed it. Knowing what her future held was a good thing – a safe thing. She wasn't one to mess men around, not Ethan *or* Martin. All she would do was drink her coffee, imagine what might have been, and then tell him straight.

This was nice, but I'm not available for anything more. She rehearsed the speech as she stepped out of her Suzuki.

A car went by and she shrank, wondering if it was someone she knew – someone who might mention seeing her to Ethan. What was she doing? What was she thinking, slinking along like a thief? Series two of her and Ethan's favourite show started that night, for God's sake. Ethan would make popcorn. How could she face him or watch him milling around the kitchen, doing his best to please her when she had spent the afternoon with another man?

She didn't hurt people. Meeting Martin for cheap thrills was cruel and unfair to him *and* Ethan. Better to get back in the car before she did something she would regret, but she couldn't just run away and leave the poor guy sitting there. What if he came back to the salon and confronted her? It was best to just meet him and be up front.

Sorry, Martin. I shouldn't have agreed to this. She mulled the words over in her mind. *Be abrupt, but honest.* Agreeing to meet him had been a spur-of-the-moment mistake and she would make him see that.

Better still, she would walk past the window and if he wasn't there yet, she would just keep going. That way if he came into the salon, she could honestly say she'd been there and then she would make up a story about how something had come up and she hadn't been able to wait.

Why didn't she get his number? It would have been so much easier if she could have texted and cancelled. Why didn't he offer his number? Strange, she thought. He didn't ask for her number or offer his. Who did that? The question gave her pause, but then she remembered his shyness and how he hadn't been able to make eye contact with her in the mirror. *Poor guy.*

As planned, she did walk by, then slowed to glance through the window. Martin was already seated and reading a book. Athletic, good-looking, and a reader; she was impressed. Successful too, she thought, remembering the Alfa Romeo. But he would no doubt turn out to be a real asshole and that would be the end of that. Probably a good thing too, she told herself as he stood and smiled as soon as he saw her enter the shop. A guy like him had to have some flaws.

Chapter Eight

There was so much she didn't know about Marty's involvement with the two men who broke into their house, but for now all she wanted was a shower and some sleep. At the same time, she doubted she'd ever sleep soundly again.

The silence in the car allowed her to concentrate on her phone and the photograph the vet had sent. Angel with a white dressing taped to his side and cheerful yellow tape covering his front legs. Body battered but spirit unbroken, smiling his goofy grin.

She knew a smile like that would have been elicited by the veterinary nurse telling him he was a good boy or something similar. If the woman only knew, Beth thought, as tears threatened to well up. Angel had saved her from God knew what. He had acted on his natural instinct to protect her and in doing so, he killed a man. Some might see Angel as a killer or a dangerous animal, but not Beth. She was grateful for her dog's actions. If possible, she loved him even more.

Angel was their compromise. Four years ago, Marty had promised her the world, but one that didn't include children. On that, Marty refused to budge. With their wedding looming, they argued. The bitter quarrels were made worse by Marty's refusal to give a solid reason for his aversion to parenthood. If he had just given her something, some speck of understanding, the recalcitrance would have been easier to swallow.

Instead, she was left to suppose – so she told herself – his reasons must have stemmed from his childhood. Wasn't childhood the root of all adult hang-ups? Whatever the cause, she felt trapped and strong-armed into an agreement she knew she would regret. In part, she believed he would change his mind. That s*he* would change his mind. They'd be so happy together that Marty would see that a child would only add to their love.

The wedding arrangements were made, a honeymoon in New Zealand booked, and a year's lease paid on the house. A nice house. What choice did she have?

'He's giving you things,' her mother had warned when she was supposed to have been admiring the expensive wedding dress. 'But are they the things you truly want?'

Why did wanting always make her think of Ethan? Ethan with his soft brown eyes and early laugh lines. Eyes filled with hurt. Pain she had carved into his once open features. She couldn't think of him, not on her wedding day. Those stirrings of longing and guilt were disloyal to the man she was about to marry.

'They're in love,' her sister Reeva had intervened. Reeva had always been quick to save the day. 'That's all that matters.'

Sweet romantic Reeva had been willing to fly from the UK to Australia to be a part of the wedding. Calm in a crisis and a font of good advice, Reeva knew how to keep a secret. Even when they were kids, Beth knew she could trust her sister to keep her confidences. Just hearing her little sister's voice would make things easier. Yes, Beth thought while staring at Angel's photo. Reeva had a knack for defusing a situation. Reeva would know what to do.

There was the time difference to consider. Beth tried to remember how it worked. Why did something as simple as working out the time difference suddenly seem like a complex equation? When the numbers finally came to her, she realised that her sister would probably be asleep or out with friends. Unlike Beth, Reeva made friends so easily.

Beth imagined Reeva sitting in an English pub surrounded by a group of people. The air would be filled with laughter and conversation. Could she drop something so horrible on her little sister? What would knowing do to Reeva's happy existence? Telling her would be like throwing a grenade into her world, which would make Reeva an accessory or at least something close to a criminal.

Sharing the terrible secret would lift the weight from Beth's shoulders, but in doing so it might shift the burden onto Reeva. Telling her would be the same as saying, 'You decide what to do.' No matter how much she craved the release of unburdening herself, Beth couldn't drag Reeva into her mess.

"I'll go in," Marty said, turning off the engine.

Beth glanced around startled to find they had reached their destination. After hours of driving and kilometres of tension, the tranquillity of the setting jarred her back into the moment.

Midday sun trailed a yellow ripple over the surface of White Mist Lake while timber cabins sitting in a semi-circle overlooked a small boat ramp, where a couple of canoes swayed against an aging dock. A lone duck reared up and ruffled its feathers. Startled by the slamming of the car door, the bird paddled to the opposite side of the bank.

On another day and at a different time, Beth might have been charmed by the idyllic retreat. But without another soul in sight, the perfect lake looked cold and bottomless and the trees appeared dark and imposing, like they were standing guard. *Couples therapy.* The words seemed incongruent with the austere setting.

Through the office window, she saw Marty talking to a woman in a cherry-red blouse. When the woman passed something across the counter, Beth caught a glimpse of the dark hair. A moment later, Marty dashed back to the car carrying a key and a stack of pamphlets.

"We've got the one at the far end. Number ten," he said. "I told the manageress we wanted privacy."

Chapter Nine

The pressure felt almost non-existent, but at least the water was hot. Beth let the shower run until her skin turned red and started to sting. Turning, she positioned herself so the spray pelted the area between her shoulder blades. Slowly, the pain turned into a dull ache, but her back was still stiff.

Leaving her clothes in a pile, she wrapped a towel around her body and returned to the bedroom. Marty didn't turn when she entered, not leaving his post at the window.

"You think he'll come looking for us?" Beth asked as she pulled on clean clothes.

When Marty didn't answer, she pulled back the covers on the queen-size bed and crawled in fully dressed. Her body ached with weariness, but her muscles refused to relax.

"Are we safe, Marty?"

She wasn't sure why she bothered asking. They both knew his days as her protector were over, but she supposed some habits died hard.

"There was a lot of blood in the kitchen," he answered without turning around. "Some of it could have been his. Angel might have got him a good one too."

"Who is he?" The words slurred as she struggled to keep her eyes open.

If an answer came, she didn't hear it. Almost asleep, it occurred to her that her body had finally decided to cooperate with her mind. For some reason she found the thought hilarious. It would be good to share a laugh again, but before she could form the words to let Marty in on the joke, she was asleep.

Lost in a deep, dreamless slumber, she surfaced and thought she heard her mother's voice close by, but muffled. Before drifting again, she heard a sharp and woeful cry. Frowning and remembering the ducks, she tucked herself deeper into the comfort of the bed and returned to the land of uncomplicated sleep.

She woke to find twilight creeping through the window, blurring the line between day and night and tinting the room in dusky hues of mauve. Sitting up, she took in the undisturbed covers on the other side of the bed and the emptiness of the room. Her first thought was that Marty had gone. That he had run away and left her to face the mess alone.

The toilet flushed and she felt a wave of emotion, but wasn't sure if the feeling was relief or something darker. She also wondered why she had been so quick to assume that Marty would abandon her.

"You're awake," Marty said as he crossed the room. "We'll wait until it's dark."

There was no need to say more. She knew he was talking about getting rid of the body. Time crawled on, with Marty restless, sometimes watching the window or staring vacantly at the TV. After a few attempts, she gave up on trying to make small talk.

"You hurt yourself," she said noticing a scratch on his hand.

"Oh, that." He stared at the cut absentmindedly. "I dropped the keys on the steps outside and they slipped through the gap. I must have scratched it when I was fishing them out."

Darkness came early in winter. By five thirty, night had fallen. Marty insisted they wear the clothes they'd had on earlier when they had handled the body. One set of fibres was better than two. Later, they planned on disposing of the clothes and anything that might link them to the body. She wondered, fleetingly, if he'd gotten the idea from a TV show or if the details were things he had learned elsewhere.

Once they were dressed, he said, "This is the last bit. After it's done, we can put it all behind us."

The last part sounded forced and disingenuous, alongside his refusal to meet her gaze. Was he lying or just feeling guilty about what he was asking her to do? Once they were on the road, there would be no turning back. She would have no choice but to go through with the plan.

"Okay," Beth said then turned her back to him, picked up her phone and shoved it down the front of her pants. "I need to use the bathroom."

After locking the door, she flipped down the toilet seat and sat. She took out the mobile and stared at the screen. It wasn't too late. Yes, she had gone along with the plan and had even helped Marty move the body, but shock and fear had driven her to do things she'd never imagined herself capable of. So far, everything could be explained to the police. It would be difficult at first, but after she explained they would see that Angel had only acted to protect her and everything after that had been panic.

With the decision made, she moved quickly and keyed in triple zero. There was a delay and a second of low static before the call went through and then she heard ringing.

"Beth?" Marty called from the other side of the door. "You okay?"

"Yes, fine," she replied and ended the call.

Holding the mobile to her forehead and squeezing her eyes shut, she felt her last chance had slipped away.

"Come on, pet," he persisted then tried the handle. "We have to do this."

She flushed the toilet and opened the door to find Marty leaning against the door frame. His eyes darted behind her to the empty bathroom.

"What were you doing in there?" There was suspicion in his voice.

"Jesus, Marty," she snapped. It wasn't difficult to feign irritation. "Can't I even use the toilet without you banging on the door?"

"You can't bring that." He pointed to her pocket. "Our movements could be tracked. Phones ping off the towers. It's too risky."

* * *

While driving toward the exit, she noticed that only one other cabin appeared to be occupied. Yellow light spilled out of its window, but there was no sign of a vehicle next to the deck. As they passed the office, the Mazda's lights picked out the grille of a car parked, not in front of the office where there were three sets of white diagonal lines carved into the bitumen, but along the far side of the building.

They drove for twenty minutes with the heater turned up against the night air. No coats allowed, not with the risk of fibres. The rational part of her felt Marty's obsession with trace evidence bordered on paranoia, but rationality was far behind them, maybe as far back as their kitchen in Perth.

As they navigated the silent road with only the endless towering trees as their witnesses, Beth thought she could actually feel Marty's neurosis in the air. Its presence was as stifling as the heat generated from the dashboard. Breathing that air made her twist her fingers and hook them like crochet needles. There was a complimentary bottle of wine in the cabin. If Marty hadn't been watching her so closely, she would have had a few sips before they left. Just enough to calm her nerves.

"The entrance to the park is on the left," Marty said, pointing at the pamphlet he'd dumped in her lap.

They were using maps because he wouldn't risk turning on the navigational system for fear it would leave a record of their movements. She didn't know whether to be grateful that he was so cautious or be worried over his state of mind.

"I read through those pamphlets," he said. "There are national parks and reserves all over the place. It's pretty much a maze of forests and bushland."

Another hundred metres along the unlit stretch, Beth spotted a patch of bitumen. A narrow scrap of grey that stood out amidst the black of the bushland.

"There!" She pointed. "Is that it?"

Marty made the turn and they bounced onto the entrance track. A few minutes later, the bitumen ended with an abrupt thump as the road petered out into little more than packed clay.

A short plank of timber no taller than a meter sat amongst the bush grass. 'Benchley Lyon's Reserve'. The letters had been burned into the mud-coloured sign.

"This is it," he said, rolling to a stop alongside the sign. "Look how crappy the sign looks. It doesn't look like this place pulls in much tourist traffic."

Further in, the track split and jutted left one way and curved right in the other direction. Without hesitating, Marty pulled right. The nose of the car skimmed the undergrowth as the trail twisted in tight bends.

"What if we get stuck?" Beth asked, clinging to the door. "What if we can't get back out?"

Her fingers were locked on the door handle as the roasting heat from the dash took her breath away. Desperate for air, she lowered the window and let the cold breeze bombard her face and hair. There was something wild about the night chill as it whispered through the dense trees – a wildness that did little to calm her nerves.

"It hasn't rained for days so the track will be solid." He gave her a sidelong glance and an impish grin. "And the forecast is for early morning showers. Rain means no tracks left behind."

Beth had to look away because if she stared at that grin for too long, she thought she might go insane.

"But it means we'll have to bury him deep," Marty continued in an almost sing-song voice.

Chapter Ten

Beth didn't know if it was her imagination, but the track seemed to have narrowed. Lush undergrowth curled out like fingers – long grey-green fingers that grabbed at the car and hemmed them in on both sides. When Marty finally stopped, there was no room to pull over.

"We'll go left," he said, letting the engine idle. "I'll time us to make sure we walk for at least ten minutes. It's unlikely anyone would stop randomly and walk that far in, so no chance of hikers finding the body."

"We're going to carry it for ten minutes?" Beth asked.

She was about to say she didn't think she could carry such a heavy weight that far, but the memory of Marty striking the steering wheel with the palm of his hand stilled her tongue.

"It's not as far as it sounds," he replied. "It'll be fine."

Beth didn't like the way he was oversimplifying what they were about to do. Struggling through thick bush with only torchlight to break up the blackness wasn't going to be fine, she thought with more than a touch of resentment. And how were they going to carry torches while hauling a dead weight? Then there was the spade and all the other gear Marty had insisted they bring along. With all his planning, he hadn't thought to include something as simple as a backpack.

"Once we find the right spot, I'll come back for the rest of the gear," he said, answering at least one of her unspoken questions.

He might have solved one of their problems, but not the issue of the torches. She tried to think, to put her fears aside and come up with a solution.

Four years ago, when she worked as a stylist, every day had been an exercise in problem solving, putting out fires and making decisions. Nothing world-shattering, but still important to the business *and* her clients.

"Is there any tape in the boot?" she asked.

Marty thought for a second. "There's a bit left on the roll. Why?"

Beth reached around and grabbed her cap off the back seat. Five minutes later she clamped it to her head and tightened the back strap. There were three torches: two small ones and a large one with a heavy cylindrical barrel. She discounted the larger one and set to work on one of the smaller ones. With a small-barrelled torch taped to the top of her cap, the headwear felt heavy, uncomfortable, and disappointingly precarious.

Biting her lip, she wracked her brain for a solution, for some way to keep the contraption in place while her hands were occupied.

"I know," she muttered while Marty looked annoyingly sceptical.

Stowing the hat between her knees, she slipped off her sweatshirt then the torn pyjamas that he had insisted she wear. Topless and shivering, she tore the pyjamas into strips.

"Beth, I don't think—"

"Just wait," she said then pulled her sweatshirt back on.

With the hat back on, she wrapped strips of fabric over the headgear and tied it under her chin to secure the contrivance in place. It still felt heavy and as uncomfortable as hell, but it would do the job. Maybe four years with nothing to think about except clothes, holidays, and keeping her body trim hadn't dulled her ability to think outside the box. Maybe there was still a spark of the old Beth smouldering under all the lavish trappings.

"My gym bag is in the boot," she said. "There should be a spare cap."

* * *

Wearing matching and equally ridiculous headgear and latex gloves, they struggled to get the body out of the boot and set it on the ground. Beth noticed that the corpse felt stiffer and easier to move. The realisation triggered her gag reflex and she coughed and swallowed until the urge to vomit had passed.

Marty, seemingly unaware of her reaction, reloaded the rest of the gear back into the boot and slammed the lid while explaining that if someone did happen to come along, they could always claim they'd stopped to pee behind a bush. If they left the spade and the rest of the equipment sitting on the track it would have been a dead giveaway. When he used the words 'dead giveaway', Beth felt a hysterical giggle bubbling in her throat.

"What's that?" she asked, noticing a dark line running between the edge of the boot and the tailgate.

Marty brushed impatiently at the spot. "Ants."

Beth grimaced. The insects must have found the body. But wasn't it too cold for ants? Before she could ask the question, Marty was bending to grasp the corpse by its shoulders.

They progressed slowly. Breaking through tangles of low-hanging vines, shrubs, and tightly clustered grass trees with only two thin shafts of torchlight was painstaking. In some places they were forced to a halt because the thick growth was impenetrable. In those instances, they had no choice but backtrack and find an easier path.

The sound of their shoes crunching on bush debris, their panting breaths and occasional groans accompanied them on the grim march. The worst was the crackle of the plastic tarp – a sound Beth knew she would hear not only in her dreams but in every quiet moment of her life.

After they were deeper into the wilds, bush lilies became more constant. With their waxy green leaves and white cones, she had always thought the wild winter flowers to be exquisitely flawless and their honey scent sweet and clean. Now they struck her as ominous signposts and their smell as cloying and sickly. The blooms' pale presence seemed like the forest itself was watching, speaking through its silence. *This way for shallow graves.*

Despite the cold, Beth sweated – a cold sweat from the effort of carrying the heavy load and keeping her chin up under the weight of the hat. Her gloves felt slick against her hands and her fingers cramped. It seemed Marty's alarm was faulty and that they'd been hiking for almost half an hour. When the watch finally sounded, she realised they'd only been walking for ten minutes.

"Thank God." She gasped, ready to set down the load.

"No." Marty's voice was sharp and breathless in the silence of the bush. "With all the back tracking we need to go further."

She wanted to argue and tell him that her arms were going numb with the effort. Beth wanted to insist that they'd gone deep enough, but she knew he was right. How far was far enough? Judging by the battle they'd had to get this far, she doubted anyone would stumble across this spot. On the other hand, they'd come this far so why not go a few more minutes and be extra careful?

"Just give me a minute," she said. "I need a break."

Exactly one minute later they moved on. This time they walked for five minutes before Marty came to a halt.

"This will do."

Beth didn't so much set the body down as drop it, trying to ignore the stiff thud when the corpse hit the ground. It was almost over, she told herself, then rubbed her gloved hands on her trackpants.

They were in a small clearing, almost enclosed by a semi-circle of shoulder-high shrubs and saplings. In sunlight it might have been quite lovely, a place to picnic or grab your honey and get down on the ground, but in the dark and with torchlight turning the foliage a ghostly silver hue, the clearing looked eerie and the trees like totems. The wrapped corpse was a grim centrepiece, disturbingly at home in the ghostly setting. There were no lilies. She was grateful for that much.

She pulled off her hat and stretched her neck while Marty bent with his hands on his knees. His spine audibly popped.

"What time is it?" she asked.

Marty's back was to her as he crouched over the body. During the hike, the tape around the corpse's head had come loose. She could hear rustling as he fiddled with the wrapping.

"Marty?"

He turned, his face a pale blur. "Just after nine."

Earlier than she had thought, but what did it matter? In a place this secluded they could take all night. Only the car wasn't hidden. It was on the track for anyone to see. The what-ifs piled up until she became desperate for the ordeal to end.

"I'll go and get the stuff," Marty said. "I won't be long. Just," – he shook his head – "just wait here."

The idea of being alone in the clearing so deep into the wilderness seemed intolerable. To stand watch over a corpse? In the dark?

"I should come with you," she said. "I can help you carry everything."

Marty stepped closer and slid his fingers around the back of her neck then pulled her close. He pressed his mouth to the top of her head. She clung to him and didn't want to let go, not because of any passionate need, but because the thought of being left in this awful place terrified her.

"It's better if you stay," he insisted then pulled away. "If I get turned around, I can call out to you and follow your voice." After seeing her expression he chuckled, and his laughter made her want to cry. "Don't worry, pet. I won't get lost. I'll be quicker with nothing to slow me down on the way to the car. Fifteen minutes there and back. Twenty tops."

He walked back into the bush and almost instantly disappeared. Beth watched the light from his torch as it moved through the trees. A few seconds and that too vanished.

Chapter Eleven

Any warmth left over from the exertion of carrying the body evaporated when Marty's light was swallowed by darkness. Beth shrugged deeper into her sweatshirt and pulled the sleeves over her hands. The fleecy fabric did little against the cold.

Torch still alight, she stripped off the tape, disengaging it from the hat. Focusing on her task, she rolled the sticky stuff into a ball and shoved it in her pocket. *Mustn't leave anything behind.* Doing something, doing anything, distracted her from acknowledging her situation. It also distracted her from the never-ending darkness and the body, not to mention the creeping belief that Marty might not return.

She wished for her phone and cursed Marty for his pedantic insistence on taking so many precautions. He was right. She acknowledged that much, but knowing that did little to dampen her frustration. A deep, dark emotion swam just beneath a shallow pool of annoyance – a feeling as deep and dark as the forest itself.

To some extent, fear and desperation had masked her resentment, but now it broke the surface. This was Marty's fault. He put her in this position. He brought the dead man into their lives. No, she thought. It went back much further than what had happened the previous night.

Marty had come along and plucked her out of her ordinary, comfortable life. He showed up in the salon all good looks and expensive clothes; charming yet insistent that she first cut his hair without an appointment and then have coffee with him.

Her life with Ethan had been happy. She'd been satisfied with their life and love, and excited by their modest plans to buy a house and, one day, start a family. Perhaps Marty smelled something on her – greed she hadn't known existed until he dangled the possibility of more under her nose. More money, more adventure, more everything. Had Marty smelt her avarice? Greedy, superficial Beth who jumped at the chance of everything Marty represented.

She clamped her teeth to stop them from chattering. Shining the light around, she saw a body twisted and brown with age. It crawled toward her and she shrieked and stepped back and almost stumbled before realising it was only a log. It was just the husk of a dried-out tree. But it *did* look alive when the beam had touched it. Just for a millisecond she thought she saw a face twisted in agony and caught beneath the gnarled edges of the wood.

"Christ," she muttered.

Wanting to sit but determined not to touch the log, she continued her search of the area. Finally, she found a hunk of branch. Not as roomy as the log, but at least it didn't morph into an undead thing when the light touched it.

It was only when she sat that she realised how exhausted she felt. Once her butt hit the wood, her body slumped. Barely able to hold her head up, her mind continued to play the blame game.

Something moved in the trees. A slow, dragging rustle, not unlike the sound a corpse might make while waking up from its deathly sleep. She twisted around, certain the body under the tarp had moved.

When the beam landed on the swaddled mass, it lay motionless. Had it moved? Was it closer than before? What if the thing under the wrapping was alive and trying to get out, slyly working its way towards her? Its cold stiff fingers uncurling as it clawed at plastic. Its fingernails working to free it from its bindings. An undead creature vengeful and intent.

How long had Marty been gone? Five minutes? It couldn't have been more than ten. He said he could make it to the car and back in twenty minutes tops, but what if he'd been wrong? He could be wandering in the dark with no idea where he was going.

She heard movement, unmistakable in the silence. Scuffing leaves paired with a thump. A solid meaty sound.

Beth sprang to her feet. "Who's there?" Her voice sounded child-like and small.

Flicking the torch around, she found the body. Its position was unchanged, but someone *was* there. She heard them moving. Maybe not someone, but something? The urge to run was powerful, it tugged at her nerves and made the muscles in her legs twitch. But where would she go? Into the blackness?

She stepped closer to the dead log then moved with halting steps and turned the light every which way until it landed on a pair of eyes. Glowing orbs fixed on her movements. Once more her mind jumped back to childhood and the Moonlight Man that lurked in the shadows.

She screamed. Not a muffled sound, but a full-bodied blast. A cry loud enough to wake the night birds from their rest and send them flapping through the trees. Something – an owl perhaps – whooshed by her face.

Arms raised and batting at wings, she tripped and fell back. The torch flew out of her grasp and rolled away. In the turning light she recognised the thing in the trees: a kangaroo, a big one. Six feet tall or so it seemed from her position on the ground.

Its muscular shoulders were tensed as the buck held Beth's gaze and sloped closer. Menacing and unafraid, the creature came further into the light, close enough for her to smell its wild scent of earthy fur and musk. He could kill her. He could tear her open with his powerful hind legs or stomp her into her own shallow grave. The irony of the situation was too cruel to contemplate.

Behind it, she saw a doe – a smaller animal, cautious and watchful. She was a trespasser in their domain. Still on the ground, she shuffled back; her movement crab-like. The buck tracked her progress while its nose twitched with interest. He held his ground and took one final sniff before turning away. With casual ease, the kangaroo moved off, dragging his thick tail over leaves and seedpods like an enormous fleshy serpent.

Beth remained in place. Dampness seeped up from the ground and soaked her pants while her breath clouded the torchlight. For some reason her thoughts were suddenly on Angel and not the roo.

Like her, Angel was probably afraid and in the dark, waiting for her to come and take him out of what must have seemed like a strange and lonely place. He'd nearly killed himself trying to protect her. Now it was her turn to do the hard stuff. Now it was time for her to pull herself together and stop behaving like a teenager in a horror film. Although, she thought while standing and brushing off her wet pants, every moment since last night had seemed like a surreal horror show.

If Marty couldn't find his way back, she would have to figure a way out of this madness on her own. She would give up on burying the body and make her way back to the car. If the car was gone, which wouldn't completely surprise her, she would walk. If getting out meant waiting until dawn, then that's what she would do. It made a lot more sense than stumbling around in the dark.

With a half-formed plan in mind, she felt a modicum of calm returning. She wasn't ready to sit on the dead log, but she did find something to occupy her time. Picking up a stick, she walked the length of the corpse and made estimations. If Marty showed up? Great! They were back in business. If not, she would cover the body with branches. Not quite a grave, but the best she could manage without a spade.

* * *

When Marty returned twenty minutes later, he appeared surprised to find her calmly waiting. She didn't waste time asking him what took so long. Instead, she nodded to the bottles of water he was carrying.

"Good. I need a drink," she said and took one of the bottles, trying not to think of how long it had sat next to the corpse in the car.

"Did you hear a scream?" Marty asked. "About twenty minutes ago?"

"No," Beth replied. "I've marked out a rectangle. The body is under one hundred and eighty centimetres long. We'll need at least a metre's width."

She couldn't blame him for his startled look. She had been acting like a panicked toddler since last night. In the last twenty-four hours, she had been a woman on the verge of cracking up. Paranoid and shrieking over every obstacle. Was it any wonder he looked surprised by her now business-like approach?

"Are you sure?" he asked. "I mean about the size because it seems big."

She re-capped the bottle and set it on the ground. "I used to cut hair for a living. I know length."

She sat on the hunk of branch and watched him dig until he was red-faced and bathed in sweat.

"You take a break," she offered. "I'll dig for a while."

There was that look again, only this time she *did* feel irritated. Was it surprising that she might be capable of something as rudimentary as digging? Did he really think she was completely helpless? However, after a few minutes using the spade, she began to wonder if his opinion of her was correct.

Knowing he expected her to throw down the spade and give up made her more determined. She dug furiously even when blisters broke out on her palms and her wedding ring ground into her finger. In the painful throes of determination, she wondered who she was trying to impress. Certainly not Marty. Not after the way he dropped his face into his hands while the man in the ski mask ripped her top open. Pausing only for a few seconds, she yanked off the ring and shoved it in her pocket.

Perhaps by moving earth in preparation for a dead man, she could also uncover the old Beth. Purposeful, organised Beth, whose days weren't being planned around gym sessions and light lunches. A woman who had responsibilities that went beyond making sure her feet were preened in readiness for sandal season.

"Okay," she said, then clambered out of the pit. "Any deeper and the whole thing will collapse on itself. We're lucky the earth's a bit damp or we wouldn't have gotten this far."

Marty, seeming not to notice that his ass was resting on a dead log that bore a remarkable resemblance to a shrivelled corpse, stood up. This time she thought she saw gratitude in his exhausted features. She was surprised for two reasons. One, he might actually be acknowledging the fact that she was able to achieve something and, two, for the first time in five years she realised she didn't give a damn what he thought of her.

Chapter Twelve

Once again, Beth took the feet while Marty grabbed the shoulders. It was only two hours since they'd set the corpse down and already it had stiffened and turned into a rigid plank. Much easier to move, but repulsive to the touch.

They shuffled sideways toward the open grave.

"On two," Marty said.

Somehow, in the pause between one and two, her gloved fingers slipped. Panicked and not wanting to drop the thing, she jerked the legs toward the hole.

The forward momentum together with the weight of the dropping legs almost pulled Marty into the grave. If he hadn't let go of the shoulders just as the feet fell in, he would have followed the downward trajectory and ended up on top of the corpse.

"Sorry, sorry." Beth gasped then grabbed Marty's shoulder. "Are you okay?"

Before he could answer, she looked into the grave and saw that the plastic wrapping had come apart, exposing the man's face. Unable to pull her eyes away, she took in the horrifying sight in one hideous gulp. Blood, matted hair, milky eyes and a glint of visible bone.

"Don't look, pet. Please don't," Marty said, taking hold of the upper part of her arms and turning her away. "You shouldn't have to see it."

He propelled her away from the hole as a fit of gagging wracked her throat.

"Sit down." He pointed at the log. "Let me cover him."

Ignoring his directions, Beth made her way to the hunk of branch and flopped down. Watery-eyed and nauseated, she felt a surge of gratitude toward Marty then dropped her head between her knees and pulled air through her nose.

Marty was no tough guy, but he *did* want to protect her. The realisation should have been comforting. Instead, it only added to her misery. Not only had she looked into the corpse's dead eyes, but now she felt like an even bigger bitch for the resentment she had been nursing. On top of that, all she could think about were her own feelings. Could the situation be any worse?

When she swallowed, the flavour of death, coppery and sweet, was on her tongue. So, yes. There was always worse. No doubt the taste was her imagination, but that didn't stop bile from rising in her throat. And what was more disgusting was knowing she had to swallow it down or risk leaving evidence at the scene.

A crime scene. No matter how she dressed it up – justifiable self-defence, a home invasion gone wrong – they were committing a horrible crime. Each thud of earth that hit Lenton Hubbard's body confirmed the nature of their crime. Added to the taste in her mouth was the creeping belief that, as the dirt hit the body, it was also burying them. Beth and Marty. Their fates were sealed. The act of concealing the body would eventually destroy them, yet she couldn't make herself stop or tell Marty to stop.

After it was over, they stripped and washed with cold bottled water. All of the clothing they'd worn was shoved in a plastic carrier bag before they redressed in clean clothes. In her mind's eye, Beth could almost envision them. Two naked figures caught in a circle of light, quivering as they carried out the final act – their pale bodies seen only by the moon. What she couldn't quite picture was how they would go on with their lives.

* * *

Fifteen minutes later they were back at the car. It was done. Mostly driving in reverse, they made their way out of the national park and then rolled toward the retreat in complete silence.

As they navigated the private road, Beth noticed the time was a little after eleven. The windows of the office building were dark, but a light was still burning in the cabin closest to it. On their left, moonlight trailed across the lake like a spectral finger. The rippling surface of the water made her feel cold while the lone cabin light added loneliness to her mix of emotions.

"Why did you choose this place?" she asked, watching the lake.

Marty took a second. "I don't know," he replied and sounded weary. "I think the advertisement said something about being secluded. I just liked the look of the lake."

* * *

"I saw a vending machine in the office," Marty said once they were back in the cabin. "I could grab us some snacks."

"The office is closed," Beth replied on her way to the bathroom. "I'm not hungry."

She didn't trust her stomach to tolerate food, but she was willing to risk the complimentary bottle of wine. The bottle, tied up with cheerful red ribbon, sat on top of the mini fridge and had been calling to her since they arrived. But the sweet relief of a drink would have to wait until she washed the feel of the grave off her skin.

"You okay?" he called after her.

There was something in his voice – not concern, but a doubtful tone that required reassurance.

"I'm fine," she said and closed the bathroom door.

* * *

With her tongue shrivelled against the roof of her mouth and moving sluggishly, she attempted to moisten her lips. The taste was like licking the underside of a crusty work boot.

She grimaced at the wine glass and the almost empty bottle on the nightstand. She wasn't really a huge drinker: a few flutes of champagne and the odd glass of white. Well, maybe she'd been having more than a few lately, but who didn't? It wasn't like she was an alcoholic.

The idea that her drinking had become too regular was too ludicrous to consider *and* funny, almost, because she didn't drink in the day. Not usually. Alcoholics drank in the day or in the morning even. She had a vague memory of sitting in bed the night before drinking glass after glass, gulping the red wine with sullen resolve.

Amidst the blurry binge, she recalled Marty's mouth, moist and urgent, devouring her neck. Did they have sex? She lifted the covers and saw that apart from a T-shirt she was naked. So, the answer was yes. They did make love, although she doubted love had factored into the act.

Sitting up and reaching under the sheet, she found her underwear and slipped it on. At that same moment a headache took up residence behind her eyes.

Marty appeared in the bathroom doorway looking quaffed and upbeat.

"You're awake," he said with a smile. "I thought I'd drive to the nearest shops and pick up a few things. Coffee? You look like you need it."

Each word dropped like a hammer pounding her brain. Tongue still useless, she gave a nod. Coffee did sound good and necessary.

She forced her unwilling mouth into action. "Something to eat."

"You take it easy," he said then moved to the bed and kissed her on the head. "I won't be long."

How could he be so chirpy? Probably because, unlike her, he didn't drink himself unconscious the night before. He probably slept like a baby, she thought with a now familiar bitterness.

"And get some decent white wine," she added.

He was already out the door; the keys jingling merrily in his fist. Not surprisingly, he hadn't invited her along on the trip to the shops. She could tell he was eager to get away – too eager. Just like Marty to ditch her and make it seem like he was doing her a favour.

Running out on errands was something of a hobby for Marty. Coffee runs, hardware needs; I-left-something-at-the-office kinds of trips. Beth always believed his need to be on the go stemmed from excessive amounts of nervous energy, but in light of what she had learned about his business dealings, or more accurately what she didn't know, she was no longer sure.

She stumbled out of bed and winced at the pain in her head and the ache in her muscles. Heavy drapes hung on either side of the window and a lacey curtain covered the centre pane. Standing to the side and peering past the thin fabric, she watched Marty stop alongside the car. He stooped and tied his shoelace.

With his shoulders hunched, he turned and looked towards the other cabins. Instinctively, she followed his gaze but saw nothing and no one. A second later, he was up and opening the car door. This time he glanced in the opposite direction toward the trees and walking trails.

Again, she followed his stare. Mist drifted around the base of the trees and turned the scenery into a bleak tangle. A secret land of hidden places and creatures. She stopped her thoughts from carrying her further into the woods.

Turning her attention back to Marty, she watched him drive away. He would visit the shops. Of this she was certain just as she knew he would return with food, coffee, and wine. Marty was a smart guy. He would have a story, something about a slow-moving cashier or a long-winded shopkeeper. What she didn't know was what else he had planned during his not-so-short errand.

It was almost thirty-six hours since the two men broke into their home and Beth still knew almost nothing about Marty's connection to the intruders. *I know where the body is buried.* Her husband, she had come to understand, was good at ducking and weaving. But he was also nervous. Nervous was an understatement. Marty was scared.

Marty's fear flat out terrified her. He might be good at ducking and weaving, but that didn't mean he hadn't bitten off more than he could chew. And worse still, some of that bite was now rammed down her gullet.

Terror made her want to call the police, but the time for coming clean had passed. Burying Lenton Hubbard had slammed that door closed. Now she had to think. Without the facts, thinking of a way out was almost impossible.

"What are you up to, Marty?" she asked, still staring out the window.

As if in answer, a duck, hidden somewhere beneath the mist on the lake, wailed out a lonely cry that echoed off the water. The sound put Beth in mind of a TV program, a period drama about an aging king. *I like it not.*

"I like it not," she said, enjoying the succinct nature of the language. The antiquated arrangement of words expressed her feelings more accurately than any modern term.

A second later she ran for the bathroom and vomited red wine until her ribs ached. Before flushing the toilet, she couldn't help but notice how the traces of wine that filled the bowl and mixed with the water as it ran in splatters down the porcelain, resembled blood. The thought set off another bout of gagging. Mercifully, there was nothing left in her stomach.

Sinking to the bathroom floor with visions of blood still making her stomach churn, a memory almost surfaced. She tried to grasp it, but couldn't quite unlock the thought. She had a feeling she was overlooking something – something important. With an aching head, the idea remained out of reach, so she let it go. Maybe it mattered, maybe not.

"I like it not," she said again and wiped her mouth with the back of her hand.

Chapter Thirteen

Washed and dressed, she felt both restless and queasy. Could a person experience cabin fever after only one night? She doubted cabin fever was the real problem. It wasn't the wooden hut that was making her jittery and unable to sit still.

Only twenty minutes had passed since Marty left and being alone made her feel vulnerable. Not that Marty would be much use if the man in the ski mask showed up, she thought with a little less bitterness now. Now it was more a sense of sadness. It had become a dull feeling of standing on the outside looking in on the past, but there was no time to examine the state of her marriage.

He's taken something that doesn't belong to him. The masked man's words kept coming back. Had the intruder's voice cracked on the word *something* or was she adding emotion where there'd been none? Was she embellishing the memory and adding in details to fit a theory? Did Marty bring that *something* with him on their nightmarish getaway? *Only one way to find out.*

Her suitcase was open in the corner of the room. Clothes were strewn over its edge and a pair of high heels – what had she been thinking? – were tossed on the rug.

No such sloppiness for Marty. His bag was neatly stowed inside the wardrobe.

Pausing to take another look through the window and check that no one was coming to kill her, she retrieved the bag and set it on the bed. A quick search revealed nothing out of the ordinary. She chided herself for thinking Marty would be dumb enough to leave a wad of stolen cash in his overnight bag. It was also ludicrous to believe that two men had gone to so much trouble over a wad of money. An overnight bag full of cash, maybe, but not a wad.

And Marty, ever the smart guy, would never leave something important enough to nearly get them both killed in a wardrobe. No, he would want to it keep close or far away in the city. She dragged her fingers through her hair. Perhaps it *was* the wooden walls that were getting to her. She needed air, but could she risk going outside?

"Paranoid," she muttered then shoved everything back into the overnight bag.

While settling the clothing, her fingers found a bulge in the bottom of the bag. Something was wedged under the flat plastic liner that sat at the base of the carryall. Not money, but something long and rigid. Disturbingly, her first thought was drugs. She pulled back the base and found a hunting knife.

Looking at the vicious blade took her back to the moment the masked man held a knife between her breasts. A moment, she knew, that would live forever in the dark recesses of her mind and maybe even grow into something sour and poisonous. Biting her lip, she stared at the weapon. It looked identical to the one Lenton Hubbard had held over Marty.

The idea of touching the thing made her skin crawl. Yet Marty had touched it. For some reason, he hadn't just handled it; he had kept it and packed it away in his overnight bag. What she couldn't fathom was why. Why keep it? Why not bury it with its owner?

If Marty intended to dispose of the blade, why hide it? Didn't hiding it change the intention into something more sinister? That can't be the case, she told herself. The knife had to be for protection. It was the only plausible explanation. She remembered how cautious he was when he left the cabin. Marty was scared. As scared as her. She had seen as much in the way he had checked his surroundings before getting in the car.

She understood his fear all too clearly because the same fear had plagued her every moment since the two men showed up in the middle of the night. The knife was Marty's way of trying to protect her. By not saying anything about the weapon, he was trying to protect her from worrying.

The weapon was grotesque, but she was grateful that he kept it for her sake. Yet, knowing he thought her too weak to handle the reality of the situation hurt. The hurt suddenly turned into anger – anger at Marty for hiding things from her. So many things. Above all else she was angry with herself. Why did she have to kill every decent thing he did with criticism? One minute she resented him for not protecting her then the next she was angry because he thought she needed protecting. Covering the blade and stowing the clothes, she returned the bag to the closet.

Still fragile from the night before, she decided that a run was out of the question, but a walk might be nice. That's what people did at bush retreats, after all.

With her jogging shoes and coat on she returned to the window. She couldn't see anything out of place. No mask-wearing strangers loitering around the lake. There were still tendrils of mist on the water, but it was early. Going outside was a risk, but if the guy in the mask wanted to get to her, he could have kicked the door in and attacked at any time since Marty left. Not really a comforting thought.

No matter how she rationalised what she was about to do, her heart was hammering when she stepped out of the cabin. A few breaths of morning air and she felt steady enough to leave the tiny deck and descend the few steps.

Aping Marty's movements, but with more subtlety, she took in her surroundings. First, she checked the other cabins. Nothing. The advertisement hadn't exaggerated when it said secluded. Deserted looked more like it. She found the quiet more than a tad unsettling, but again it was early, although early wouldn't account for the lack of cars. She also noticed that the office was closed.

A light breeze lifted her hair. Fresh clean air blew on her cheeks. Her shoes crunched on damp sand as she made her way across the bank and onto the small jetty. She didn't remember hearing rain fall during the night, but she had been pretty drunk. On the jetty her footfalls sounded hollow and overly loud on the ancient wood as the water beneath it lapped against the struts.

Looking over the lake, she began to relax. The mist had mostly lifted, leaving the water rippling under the wind as wisps of vapour drifted upwards, where they dissipated like ghosts. She decided the walk could wait. There was nowhere to sit so she dropped to the edge of the jetty and let her legs dangle above the water.

In that moment she was almost able to quell the fears that clamoured and competed for her attention. Fear of the masked man was always at the forefront of her mind, but now she had other concerns. Beth was uncertain about her future and most of that uncertainty was focused on Marty. There was a startling new side to his personality that had been mostly hidden from her until yesterday. Maybe from himself too, although something told her that wasn't the case. The enraged man screaming and pounding the steering wheel was as much an intruder in her life as the men who had broken into her house. But was he the real Marty?

Watching the calming swirls the birds made, she saw that a few geese and a pair of black swans had joined the ducks. Seeing them glide over the rippling water helped to soothe her nerves. The cool breeze suddenly kicked up a notch and rustled bushes to her right.

She glanced toward the greenery and noticed something between its leaves. Grateful for the distraction, she left the jetty and moved back to the bank to have a closer look.

The bushes were shoulder-high, tightly clustered and occupied the area between the narrow sandy bay and the grassy banks that led to the walking trails. Stepping back onto the sand, she followed the bay to an area between the bushes and the water.

On closer inspection, she found not a flower, but a scrap of something caught in the branches. Something cherry-red that fluttered as wind pelted the surrounding shrubs. Barely noticing that the sand bank was becoming narrower and the soggy ground sucked at her joggers, she moved closer.

As the lake lapped at her ankles, she took a few more steps. The scrap was almost within her grasp when she realised it was a piece of fabric – a red swatch no bigger than a butterfly. As she reached out to grab it, the wind dislodged it from the bush. Like a butterfly, it fluttered upward and toward the water then dipped and almost skimmed the lake before swirling upward again and further out over the water. A second later, it veered right and disappeared into the mist.

A few metres out, a dark shape broke the surface of the lake. Distracted from the fabric, Beth watched an oblong shell appear. It glided over the surface then sank. A snake-necked turtle hunting injured birds, no doubt. As she watched, more shells surfaced then moved slowly as they tumbled over each other then disappeared into the depths. The hungry, slimy creatures made her grimace with disgust.

When something cold touched her ankle, she let out a frightened croak and looked down to find her shoes were sodden with lake water. Without noticing, she had wandered into an area that sat hidden from view of the cabins on this side of the lake. Shivering with disgust, she danced backwards until she cleared the water.

She wasn't sure what had creeped her out more: the lake, the turtles or the cold water on her skin. Once she recovered her calm, she didn't think about the slimy creatures, only about the scrap of fabric. Plodding back to the bank, she couldn't help wondering what it was about the scrap of material that bothered her. When the office came into view, it jogged her memory. The previous day she had watched Marty check into the retreat and she remembered catching a glimpse of a woman through the office window – a woman in a cherry-red blouse.

* * *

While standing in front of the office door looking at the Tripadvisor sticker in the left-hand corner, she tried to figure out what she hoped to achieve. So what if there'd been a bit of red fabric caught in a bush? Did it have to mean something? No, she told herself, but in her new world of dead bodies and knife attacks she couldn't be sure. She'd simply go in, use the vending machine, see the woman with the dark hair, and that would be it. Case closed and she could go back to fretting about more important matters.

As she entered, an old-fashioned shop bell that hung from the door tinkled. A prickle of unease touched the base of her neck as the man behind the counter looked up from the papers he'd been sorting and smiled.

God, how she wished she'd rehearsed something before opening the door.

"Morning." The guy nodded to the window. "Clear skies today."

He waited for a response, so she gave a grin that felt too stretched. "Yes, beautiful day," she said. He seemed to be expecting more so she pushed on. "I meant to ask the lady who checked us in yesterday about the Wi-Fi password." It was the best she could come up with on the hop, but it sounded plausible.

"Oh, yes," he replied and took a slip of paper from under the desk. "Here you go. That will get you in."

Beth stood her ground and reached for the paper while keeping some distance between them. Over the man's shoulder, a heavy curtain partially hid a back room. Somewhere beyond the curtain a radio played.

"Is she around?" Beth asked. "The woman that checked us in?"

The man's smile morphed into concern. "Is there a problem with your cabin? Because I can—"

"No. No." The words came out too abruptly. "It's just that she mentioned we might see geese on the lake," she said, making the story up on the spot. "I wanted to let her know that there are a few out there today."

So far, she thought she sounded casual, but before she could stop herself, she blundered. "Is she here?"

It was the second time she had asked the same question and she half-expected the guy to call her out on it. *Why do you keep asking about the woman? Are you obsessed with her?*

"No, sorry," he answered unfazed. "She's gone to Bunbury to visit a friend."

His eyes were blue, light under dark brows. He appeared to be in his mid-forties, but he wore a patterned jumper that looked like it belonged on someone much older. He would have been attractive if not for his woeful fashion sense. Her mind jumped to Marty and his impeccable trendy jeans and jackets.

"I'll let Tracy know when I call her tonight," he continued.

For an instant, she was confused and not sure what he was talking about.

"The geese," he prompted. "She'll be pleased to hear they're back."

"Okay, yes." She wasn't sure how to end the conversation. Her mind was on geese, white birds, and cherry-red fabric. *Flesh and blood.* Then, like a gift from the gods, she remembered the vending machine Marty had mentioned. Glancing around, she saw it against the far wall.

"I'll just grab a snack," she said more to herself than to the man.

Realising she was still holding the slip of paper with the Wi-Fi password, she shoved it in her pocket and that simple action brought back the memory she'd been searching for earlier in the cabin. The feeling she was missing something now clarified into razor-sharp horror. All thoughts of the woman in the red blouse were quickly forgotten.

She stood frozen in place with her hand in her pocket and her mouth agape. She could see the man behind the counter watching her, probably clocking the bruise on her face and pegging her as a loony. A Mickey Rooney as her mother would say.

She knew she should say something, but the gravity of her mistake left her dumbfounded. With the man's eyes trained on her, she turned and fled the office; her wet shoes squelching as she went. If he came around the counter and watched through the window, he would see her sprinting for the cabin, but she didn't care.

Chapter Fourteen

"Sorry. I got caught up behind a bloke who was having a nervous breakdown over his credit card at—"

"Where are the clothes?" Beth didn't bother trying to keep desperation out of her voice.

Marty, carrying takeaway coffees, a couple of shopping bags hooked over one arm, looked confused. "What?"

"The clothes. The ones we wore last night." Beth rolled her hands in the air with her fingers splayed. "The ones you put in the plastic bag."

"In the boot. I'll get rid of it tonight. It's too risky during the day," he said.

"Good. That's good. Give me the keys," she said then held out her hand.

He set the coffees on the table next to the TV, but made no move to produce the car keys.

"What's going on?" His voice sounded flat and his eyes had taken on the same warning look he had given moments before he lost his temper and had pounded the steering wheel. Not for the first time that morning she experienced a prickle of unease. She chose her next words carefully.

"My wedding ring. I took it off when I was digging and I'm pretty sure I put it in the pocket of the pants I was wearing."

Marty's expression was unreadable. For a moment he said nothing. "You're pretty sure?" he asked.

"I'm sure," Beth said without hesitating. "That's what I did."

She was still speaking when he turned and left the cabin. Beth watched from the doorway as he went to the boot and grabbed the bag. No careful checking of the area this time, not so much as a glance. Either he thought the danger had passed or in his single-mindedness he had forgotten to be wary.

Without a word, he closed the cabin door and then he upended the bag, spilling clothes, hats, and rubber gloves onto the rug. Before she could move, he was on his knees sifting through the pile. He found the pants and dug into the pockets then tossed a wad of balled up tape onto the floor. He found a few scraps of fabric in the other pocket which he dumped on the rug.

He was yanking the pockets inside out when Beth joined in the search. Instead of the clothes, she grabbed the plastic bag hoping the ring had fallen out of the pocket and was somewhere at the bottom of the carrier. They continued for a few more minutes, their movements growing frantic as it became clear that the ring was gone.

Finally, she sat back on her heels and rubbed her fingers against her temples. The ring wasn't amongst the clothes. While waiting for Marty to return, she had already searched the cabin even though she was positive she'd been wearing the ring last night.

"Maybe it fell out in the boot," she said with little hope.

Marty looked at her for a moment. It was an accusing stare – one that said she had fucked everything up. They both knew their initials were engraved on the inside of the wedding band. Not a smoking gun exactly, but enough to be a problem if Lenton Hubbard was ever found and linked to Marty.

Marty stood and kicked the pile, sending clothes in all directions. Air and fabric skimmed her face as his foot flew within centimetres of her cheek.

"Damn it, Beth," he grunted as if she'd been the one who had almost kicked him in the face.

Turning on his heels, he headed back to the car. This time Beth followed and watched as he swatted ants off the bumper before opening the boot. Her gym bag was shoved into the corner. The only other items were the spade and torches. He made quick work of the search, but came up empty.

"We'll have to go back," he said once they were back inside. He didn't need to say more. They both knew he meant back to where they'd buried Lenton. "But not tonight."

She could see he was angry and knew she should apologise. The ring was her mistake and he was waiting for her to say so. An apology cost nothing and might calm him down, but she couldn't bring herself to give him what he wanted. It was petty of her, yet she relished the idea of withholding the apology, telling herself that he was the one who had dragged them into this mess, so sorry should be his word and not hers.

His shoulders were stiff and his mouth tight. He was tense, stuffing clothes back into the bag with agitated movements. With each new obstacle and every sickening bump in the road, he was pulling further away from her. She knew this, yet did nothing to close the void.

"Your coffee is getting cold," he said before carrying the bag back to the car.

She took the lid off one of the coffees and took a few sips. Despite Marty's anger and the seriousness of the situation with the lost ring, she was hungry. In one of the shopping bags, she found croissants, a couple of raw steaks, a loaf of crusty bread, and a bottle of wine. In another she found milk, teabags, and a small jar of instant coffee. How long did he think they were going to stay?

Standing at the window, she bit into one of the pastries and watched the lake. *I like it not.* The words repeated over and over in her mind.

"Why are you wearing your coat?" Marty asked when he stepped back into the cabin. "Did you go somewhere while I was gone?"

It wasn't a conversation starter so much as an accusation, so she took her time chewing and swallowing before she spoke.

"Did you see the woman that checked us in when you were leaving?" she asked, answering his question with one of her own.

Marty picked up his coffee and sat on the bed. He looked calm now, his body relaxed. The constant ups and downs of his moods were becoming increasingly unsettling.

"Um…" He took a sip of the hot brew. "I think I saw her when I drove out this morning. Why?"

She couldn't say how she knew, but she was sure he was lying.

"I wanted to ask her if it's okay for us to use the canoes." The fictional reason came quickly and she marvelled at how swiftly she'd adapted to lying. But that wasn't true. She turned into a liar five years ago, not long after she first met Marty.

"You don't have to ask, pet," he said, sounding relaxed. "They're for the guests to use, but it's not the weather for a canoe ride. That wind will tip you over and dump you in the freezing water."

"I'm going for a walk," she said.

"Do you want me to come?" He sounded less than enthusiastic.

"No." She turned and gave him a smile she hoped looked breezy. "Eat your croissant and take it easy for a while. I'm just going to stretch my legs."

With her phone in her pocket, she avoided the lake and headed toward the walking trails where the ground between the trees was rust-coloured and shiny from the rain. Her feet were damp and cold inside her wet socks and shoes, but it felt good to be outside and away from Marty's fluctuating moods. It was a relief to breathe clean air instead of oxygen heavy with unspoken tension.

There was a patch of sand and a swing set at the foot of the trail. The swing's recycled rubber seats danced in the breeze. As they moved, the chains made a grinding sound that reminded her of screams. Playgrounds were strange places: lively and wonderful when filled with children, but mournful and eerie when deserted.

With her head down and watching where she stepped, she gave the swings a wide berth and stepped onto the trail that led east and deeper between the trees. Her feet were sodden and her hands had become numb with the cold. But the cold was good. It helped clear her headache and clarify her thoughts.

She thought of how frantic Marty had been over the loss of her ring and yet he didn't want to go back and search the burial site right away. Why wait? Also, she assumed he owed the intruders money, but Marty hadn't really confirmed anything outside of a vague reference to drugs. Then there was the second man in the ski mask. Would he be back?

She needed answers, but there were other matters to consider, like her own plans. Something was forming in her mind: a plan that didn't involve Marty. Could she really do it? Cut and run? Three days ago, she would have said she couldn't live without her husband. Now, she wasn't so sure.

Why should she stay? They had done what they came to the retreat to accomplish. Why hang around? The whole place gave her the creeps. Worse than the creeps. It set her nerves on edge. Something was off at White Mist Lake. The place had an almost surreal quality that made her want to scream just to hear something truly real – something that would shatter the false tranquillity.

She stopped walking and listened, almost certain she'd heard something that sounded like echoing footsteps. Yet, an echo was impossible on soft damp ground amongst thick foliage.

With her breath fogging the air, she waited. Apart from the swings creaking as they swayed in the wind, there was only silence. She spotted a spider's web splayed out among the branches of a sapling gum. Dewy droplets turned the web into a prism of colour between the yellow and orange legs of a giant orb spider.

"No one here but us," she whispered to the spider then felt foolish.

Had she heard something? Footfalls? Marty?

Breathing hard, she forced herself to turn around. There was nothing but red dirt and trees. Rather than make her fears seem silly, the absence of movement and noise left her feeling more at risk: more exposed and alone. Not just in this hollow place, but in her marriage and her life. The discontentment had been festering long before two men had shown up with their knives.

Her life with Marty was a pretty wilderness filled with dinners, holidays, clothes, cars, and sex. He called her pet, which was something she'd always found sweet, but now she realised it wasn't sweet, but an indictment of her place in his life. She was an attractive pet that kept his house *and* bed warm; an accessory worn on his arm.

Looking around, she spotted a tree stump and flopped down. It wasn't Marty's fault. He tried. He gave her what she wanted. Almost. He'd moulded himself into the perfect husband, but even that was a lie. In truth he was far from perfect.

God, what a mess. A steaming hot disaster. A catastrophe she was close to being done with. Done with the housewife thing and done with the loneliness. Tears fell, warm on her cold cheeks and quickly turned into sobs.

Marty wasn't the only one with vacillating moods. Her emotions were like a coin flipping in the air. Like a shiny disc that landed sometimes on overwhelming love, sometimes on resentment or fear or hate. She was dizzy from the deluge of emotions.

Unexpectedly, she experienced a sudden and overpowering longing to hear her mother's voice and to see the soft curves of her face. They'd been close once. But things had changed when Beth had announced her intention to marry Marty.

After the conversation about Marty giving her *things*, she and her mother drifted apart. Their relationship changed into something that on the surface resembled closeness, but had lost its depth. The thread that once drew them together through good times and rough patches had snapped.

Two years ago, her mother moved to Albany. There was a time when Beth would have been devastated at the mere thought of the two of them being separated by a six-hour drive, but when the move came, she felt surprisingly relieved.

'Paulette has friends in Albany. She needs a bit of company,' Marty had said in his this-is-for-the-best voice.

Beth had eagerly agreed, wanting to distance herself from the growing rift. The distance would free her from the awkward visits, watching her mother fidget and refold tea towels or wipe already spotless counters; anything to avoid that awful meeting of their eyes. Eyes that reflected unspoken hurt and resentment. It comforted Beth to know she wouldn't have to avert her gaze when they spoke on the phone. But she couldn't guard her voice and even that took on a hard edge.

Now she wanted nothing more than to throw herself into her mother's arms and let her mother rub her shoulders the way she had when Beth was a child. She wanted to unburden herself and tell Paulette what they'd done, but telling the truth would be the same as admitting that her mother had been right about Marty. He was no good for her and all he could offer were superficial trappings with no substance. Deep down Beth had known it from the beginning. She resented her mother not because Paulette disliked Marty, but because Paulette had been right about him.

Some minutes later, Beth took out her phone and did what she'd come to do.

"Hi, it's Beth Jacobsen. I'm calling about my dog, Angel."

A moment later Beth was connected to a vet nurse.

"He's doing well, eating and being a sweetie with the staff." The woman's voice dropped into a more serious tone. "He's missing his mum."

The tears returned and Beth struggled to keep them out of her voice. "I'll be picking him up tomorrow. Probably late afternoon if that's okay?"

It was arranged. She'd leave in the morning although she hadn't figured out the transportation part. A three-hour drive back to Perth to pick up Angel. At some point she'd call her mother and ask if she could stay with her until she got back on her feet. The answer, Beth knew, would be an enthusiastic yes.

Beth stowed the phone and headed back toward the lake. *What about the dead man?* a tiny voice asked. What about the lost ring? They were reasonable questions, ones that had her gazing up at the treetops as they swayed under an unsympathetic sky.

What was done couldn't be undone. Had she read that somewhere? Lenton Hubbard was dead and his body disposed of in a not-so-shallow grave. She'd have to learn to live with her crime or at least find a way to make up for it.

An unbidden memory surfaced of her in a blue bikini, the one with the tiny white birds racing over the fabric. Marty reclined on a rug. They were on the banks of the Swan River estuary, wet from swimming and still breathless as they shared an orange. Her lips were coated in the cold, sweet juice of the orange as Marty ran a strand of her hair between his fingers, squeezing out trickles of water. The memory of that day was crisp and shiny, somehow clearer than any other moment in her life.

'I know it's been hard on you, but we've turned a corner now. We'll be happy and we won't need anyone else.' His eyes were shiny and his skin tanned as the setting sun tinged his face with golden light.

'You're my home now, Beth. I'll always take care of you. You believe me, don't you?'

She did believe him and loved him. Not a sweet love, but a fierce one that made it difficult for her to speak. He was hers. A man like Marty wanting and loving her seemed like an impossible dream that had come true.

When they kissed, she tasted oranges and salt water and there was a sense that nothing could touch them. Later, after the wedding she thought of that moment and turned it over and over in her mind. While lying in bed, she had relived the power of his words. His vow that day meant more than the ones they had made in front of the marriage celebrant.

That man on the riverbank was *her* Marty – a man who needed her, and only her. Could she leave him? Could she turn her back on him because of the things he'd done and the danger he had dragged into their lives? Did that kiss still linger? *Oranges and salt.* Had the cleanliness of that taste been soured by the blood on their hands? Soured beyond recovery? She didn't know and felt exhausted by the weight of her thoughts.

How long had she been standing with her hands in her pockets staring up at the trees? Twenty minutes according to her phone. A strange thing to do: stand in thought and lose track of time like that. Or maybe her mind had simply zoned out to escape the strain of knowing she'd committed an unthinkable act. She convinced herself of these things, not wanting to revisit her earlier thoughts of hell and the surrealist quality of White Mist Lake.

While hurrying back, she saw the cabin and felt a crawling sensation in her gut, which she recognised as dread. She was developing an aversion to the cabin and its parched walls. Instead of turning onto the gravel path that led to the hut, she walked toward the office.

The tinkling bell reminded her of old shops and hotels; the kinds of places she'd only seen in films. This time the counter was unattended giving her the opportunity to look around. A computer sat on the other side of the counter, something of an anachronism in the almost antique setting.

Behind the counter she could see the back room. No radio softening the mood now. Alone and unobserved she stepped up to the desk. Papers were scattered on the nook that was built into the other side of the counter, next to a dark green rotary telephone. There was no trace of the woman that had checked them in, but why would there be?

"Hi." Taking her by surprise, the man appeared from behind the curtain.

Beth stepped back as though she'd been caught doing something underhanded, although all she'd done was stand at the counter. The bell had tinkled when she opened the door so it wasn't like she was sneaking around, not really.

"Hi," she said. "I'm Beth. We met this morning."

"Yes, cabin ten. Easy to remember seeing as you're the only guests. I'm Craig Williams and this" – he spread his arms to take in the computer and the counter – "is a total mystery to me."

Seeing her confusion, he quickly continued. "I'm covering for my sister, but it's not my usual job. The office is Tracy's gig. You could say I keep the place running. Maintenance and gardening, not this side of things. But how hard can it be?" he asked while looking at the computer.

"Right." Beth was taken aback by Craig's candour. She was also surprised that the check-in woman, Tracy, was his sister and not his wife. Somehow, she had pegged them as a husband-and-wife operation. "Did Tracy say when she'd be back?"

Craig shrugged. "She didn't say anything. I came out here to look at the taps in cabin three and found a note saying she was going to stay with a friend for a few days." He gave a tired sigh. "I'm not surprised. This can be a lonely place. It's not good for her to be out here on her own for too long. God knows I get it. Just a bit of a heads up would have been nice."

Beth wanted to ask more questions but feared her queries would sound oddly specific and probing. In her situation she couldn't afford to set off any alarm bells. The questions had to be subtle and casual.

"If you need help with anything" – she gestured to the computer – "I'm happy to lend a hand." Before he could refuse, she pushed on. "I used to use an online booking system when I worked in a salon, so I know it takes some getting used to."

Craig scratched his neck. "Okay. Yes, if you have time. I can't see anything booked for this week so maybe I'm looking in the wrong place. I was going to ring Tracy, but if she's taken off, it means she needs time away from this place. Best to leave her for a few days and let her sort herself out."

There was something in the way he talked about his sister; a tired resignation that made Beth think that Tracy had taken off before. Maybe more than taken off. Her gut told her that Tracy might be having a few problems coping with White Mist Lake Retreat.

Beth took off her coat while Craig left her to it and went in the back to make coffee. The booking site was similar to the one she was familiar with. Easy to navigate, but not intuitive unless you knew what you were doing. A few minutes of poking around and she was on the bookings page.

Surprised by what she found, she took her hands off the keys and stared at the screen. Craig was correct. There were no bookings for this week, but there had been plenty. All of them had been cancelled, yet someone had been in cabin one when they drove out of the retreat last night.

On further investigation, she saw that cabin ten had been booked under the names David and Beth Freeman. How, she wondered, in an age of credit cards had Marty been able to pull off using fake names? Trust him to find a way around such things. Frowning, she also noted that their cabin had been booked not for three days, but five.

"Coffee's ready," Craig called from the back room.

Still thinking about the cancellations – seven in all – and the fake names, she minimised the bookings screen. It wasn't until she was in the doorway that led to the back that she hesitated. She didn't know Craig and had only met him that morning, yet she was going into a back room with him. Even the words 'back room' had an unsavoury sound to them.

From where she stood, she could see part of the living quarters. A homely looking sitting room with two sofas, a stand-up lamp, a television, and a side cabinet. There was also a coffee table where Craig had placed two cups.

"Can we have the coffee out here?" she asked. "I can run you through the bookings."

Was it disappointment she saw on his face? It was difficult to tell because he was sitting just beyond the reach of the lamplight.

"Good idea," he said.

He brought another stool from somewhere in the back and they sat side by side. Beth ran him through the cancellations then how to enter new bookings according to date.

"Didn't your sister explain all of this?" she asked then sipped coffee.

Craig chuckled. "Several times, but never as simply as you just did. Tracy's not much of a teacher and I'm not the best student."

"Do you live here? You and Tracy?" she asked trying to keep the conversation on Tracy.

"God, no. Too many memories for me," he replied. "We own the place, but I live in Bunbury. I'm usually here three times a week. I only came by last night to drop Tracy's car off. She let me use it while mine was being repaired."

Beth set her cup on the desk nook. "I saw a light on in cabin one last night. Was it you?"

"Yeah. I found Tracy's note so I slept in the cabin. I use the living quarters here during the day, but if a cabin's available, I take it." He gave Beth a what-are-you-going-to-do look. "It beats sleeping in my sister's bed, which is in my parents' old room."

It seemed that before leaving, Tracy had cancelled seven bookings. It made sense if she *had* been feeling overwhelmed. The snatch of red fabric and the way it fluttered on the wind came to mind and made Beth wonder what else Tracy was struggling with.

"I didn't have anything with me," Craig continued. "So I ended up digging one of my father's jumpers out of a box in the store room. If I don't hear from Tracy by tomorrow, I'll have to drive back to Bunbury and pick up a few things."

So, Craig's fashion sense wasn't as heinous as Beth had first imagined. She started to say something to that effect when an idea hit her. If she did go through with leaving, she could snag a lift with Craig.

She wouldn't have to give him all the details. There was plenty of time to make up an excuse for leaving without her husband. Something about work commitments maybe. It would come to her. Why not? She was becoming quite the liar.

"Do you mind me asking how you hurt your face?" he asked, taking her by surprise.

Great liar that she'd become, she kicked herself for not foreseeing the question and having a story ready. Without meaning to, she touched her face.

"My dog was panicked by a loud noise. He jumped through the kitchen window and I was injured," she said, not wanting to meet Craig's gaze.

Even to her own ears the story sounded crazy, but hopefully crazy enough to be believable.

"Jesus." He seemed genuinely shocked. "Is he okay?"

She was touched by Craig's reaction and his immediate concern for Angel's well-being. Then, to her horror, tears sprang into her eyes.

"Yes, he's fine." She almost knocked over her coffee in her haste to stand. "Look, I have to get back before Marty sends out a search party," she said and grabbed her coat.

"Sorry." He was on his feet, following her to the door. "I didn't mean to upset you. Are you okay?"

"You didn't," she said on her way out. "Thanks for the coffee."

"Are you sure you're—"

She pulled the door closed behind her, cutting off further questions.

Chapter Fifteen

"Nice walk?" Marty asked, but the pleasantness in his voice sounded disingenuous.

"Cold," she said as she shrugged off her coat. She had learned something from her time with Craig. Marty had lied about seeing Tracy that morning. What she didn't know was why.

Later that evening they sat on the back deck. Marty was cooking the steaks on the barbeque while Beth sat in a plastic chair, already two glasses into a bottle of wine. The smell of cooking meat made her hungry and disgusted at the same time.

She held up her glass and watched Marty through it and was startled by the ferocity of her feelings. Anger flared from somewhere deep and dark. It was a seasoned resentment, much older than that which she had experienced over the last two days. Its flame burned hot and long, sparked by the choice he pushed on her, which was no choice at all. It was bitterness stoked by old wounds.

He had forced her to give up a dream she'd barely known she harboured until he wrestled it out of her arms. He knew what he was doing. Marty was a smart guy. He deliberately waited until the wedding was booked and then he threw out the demand. He manipulated her then, just like he was manipulating her now.

Blood swelled in her ears and pounded the same word over and over. *Liar.* It would be easy to jump up from where she sat and fling her drink into his lying face, glass and all.

Love and hate. Orange and salt.

"What did you take, Marty?" she asked, enunciating each word with deliberate precision.

He looked up from the grill. A carefully crafted mask of confusion creased his features. It didn't fool her.

"You know what I'm talking about," she insisted before he could respond. "Tell me now or I'm leaving."

Something murky settled in his eyes. She'd seen the look before and knew she should tread carefully, but there was also a part of her that wanted things to turn ugly – the excruciating pleasure of dragging the mess into the light. She wasn't afraid. The booze quelled her fears and made her limbs pleasantly numb. It briefly occurred to her that the booze could become a problem, but the concern was fleeting.

Marty turned and planted his feet wide apart. He was thinking. Her eyes moved to his hand and the still fresh scratch – the one he said he'd gotten from fishing the keys out from the gap under the front step. Something about the scratch bothered her. It stirred something, but in the heat of the moment the thought was lost.

"Money," he said in a tone that suggested it was of no importance. "A bit over one hundred and fifty thousand."

She wasn't sure if he was telling the truth or even a part of it.

"And that's what they wanted? Money?" she asked.

If Marty was telling the truth, it made sense that he didn't want the police involved. That sort of money didn't come from small-time crime. Whatever he was involved in was serious and serious crime led to serious prison time.

"The money is mine." He turned back to the barbeque and jabbed at the meat with the tongs. "I funded their operation. I drip fed the money into certain businesses until it was clean enough to use. They didn't know what they were doing until I stepped in. I was owed that money, so I took it." His voice was flat and alien-sounding.

"So, now you just give it back and these people will forget that you stole from them?" she asked around an incredulous laugh.

"Something like that," he answered.

She didn't like where this was going. Two days ago, he promised to give back whatever he took and make everything right. Something had changed.

"What does that mean?" she asked.

"That was when there were two of them."

Beth drained her glass, poured a bit more in, then took a long swallow. "Let me get this straight because I'm not sure I'm hearing you correctly. You financed something? The two men, Lenton Hubbard and the other one..." She snapped her fingers. "What's his name?"

"Joe Pike," he answered, still concentrating on the meat.

"Joe Pike and Lenton Hubbard did the dirty work. Drugs, I'm guessing. You took more than your share and so Joe and Lenton broke into our house and tried to rape me at knife point in front of you. Is that what happened, Marty? Is that what happened while you had me believing you were a mortgage broker?" On the last word her voice cracked with anger. "Am I understanding the situation?"

"I didn't think they'd involve you," he said without looking at her.

"Oh, well, then in that case there's nothing to worry about." Her words were slurred, but her temper wasn't dulled. In fact, she couldn't remember ever feeling so angry or vicious.

"You lying bastard. You selfish, greedy fuck." She tried to think of something ugly and more hateful than a string of obscenities. "I should have never left Ethan for a liar like you. This is your mess, not mine. I hope your mate Joe Pike kills you."

Marty moved with speed she hadn't known he possessed. The tongs dropped as he crossed the distance between them and dragged her to her feet so suddenly that the glass slipped out of her hand and smashed on the deck.

"Shut your mouth." His fingers dug into the flesh of her upper arms as he shook her and bit off his words through clenched teeth. "All you've done since this started is complain and nag. *What have you done, Marty? I'm not a criminal, Marty,*" he mimicked with his face only centimetres from hers. "You hated living in that shit box of a flat. You liked spending my money. You couldn't wait to get your hands on it. But now it's too dirty for you and that's *my* fault?"

He let her go with a shove that sent her stumbling back and into the chair. "You're a mean sloppy drunk, Beth, and I'm sick of the sight of you."

He stormed inside, slamming the door behind him. Too stunned to move, she listened when a minute later the Mazda roared to life and its wheels skidded over the gravel. As the sound of the car's departure faded, her anger drained into shock and humiliation. Huddled in the chair with her vision blurred by tears, she watched the meat shrivel and blacken on the grill.

Chapter Sixteen

Five years earlier

"Don't do this, Beth. Don't look at me like I'm a stranger. This isn't you. You're not in love with him." Ethan swallowed. "I don't care what's happened between you and him. We can sort it out."

Ethan looked pale and disbelieving. When she didn't respond, he tried again. "It's still us!"

She turned away, unable to look at the pain in his eyes. He didn't deserve this. None of this was his fault, yet she was doing it: hurting him, leaving him, stepping over him because Marty was waiting. And although she felt emotion welling up inside her, she was oddly disconnected from it. Her words and actions felt like an out-of-body experience.

"Don't," she said, but what she meant was don't make this hard for me.

She packed, taking only essentials. Photos, knickknacks and a few souvenirs; two years of accumulated memories that were once so precious were left behind. She was shedding her old life as if it was a jacket that had become too tight and restricting.

"You don't have to leave. You said yourself you've only known him for a few months," Ethan continued. "It's crazy to throw everything away."

The pain in his voice made her angry – angry because it reflected her cruelty and her failure as a human being.

"What about the money?" he asked.

He was referring to their savings. They had been saving for a year, putting money away for a trip to Bali. Hours spent talking about white-water rafting, parasailing, and massages by the pool. Months spent dreaming of cocktails and golden sunsets.

"Keep it," she said over her shoulder.

"You can't mean that. None of this makes sense. Can't you at least look at me?" he begged.

"Stop." She almost screamed the word as she pushed past him. "I can't breathe in this shitty flat."

Her words dropped on him like a bomb. Ethan winced. Physically he was a big man, but he appeared to shrink before her very eyes. She hated him for loving her even after she had broken his heart. Her behaviour was ugly and selfish. If she could just escape the flat, she'd be able to wipe the ugliness from her memory and cover it with a new life. The real cruelty would have been dragging it out. Keeping up the pretence and leaving him in the dark was far worse than what she was doing.

They talked for hours, her and Marty, but it always came back to one simple truth. They were in love. Ethan was a product of a life that no longer made sense. She had a right to live her life however she saw fit. She owed it to herself to live without apology or guilt. *Life wasn't always fair.* With Marty's advice ringing in her ears, she opened the front door and left Ethan behind without a goodbye.

By the time she climbed behind the wheel, she was sobbing. People broke up all the time. It's part of life, she told herself. Everyone goes through heartbreak, that's what makes real love more precious. In time Ethan would see that she'd done the right thing. He'd find someone who would make him happy. As happy as Marty has made me, she thought as she grabbed a tissue from the glove box and blotted her tears.

Chapter Seventeen

Marty's contempt, the sting of his words, and her own vile diatribe swirled in her mind like a sickening dance of cruelty. The verbal brutality had exposed long-harboured resentments. All the bitterness was laid bare, leaving her feeling naked and wretchedly alone.

She rubbed her arms. The flesh still smarted from his fingers. He had hurt her, not just with words but with his hands. It could have been worse. She knew he was capable of worse, but he had promised. He'd sworn he'd never hurt her again. The broken promise was a deeper pain: a gut-wrenching wound that made her shiver with misery.

She remembered another night, another dinner and another loss of control. A stupid argument over a pair of designer sunglasses. Angel, only fourteen months old at the time, had taken Marty's sunglasses and chewed them into a mangled mess. It would have been funny if not for Marty's anger. On a better day they would have rolled their eyes at each other and *found* the funny side.

But it wasn't a better day. Marty was mad and she, a bit tipsy and resenting his anger over something so petty, had laughed in his face. She made a nasty remark under the guise of glibness; a half-joking comment about how a baby would have been less destructive. She'd been dropping similar comments for weeks, baiting him, wanting to wound him so he'd see how much she'd given up.

In the moment, she had enjoyed the way his face flushed with anger. There was something deliciously satisfying about his loss of control. The satisfaction lasted right up until the moment he hit her.

Even now as she sat on the deck and sniffed back tears, she could still hear the flat thumping sound the back of his hand had made when it connected with her cheek. She felt the ghost of that blow still burning her skin.

That slap diminished her. It stole a part of her soul. The injury wormed its way into a place deep inside where she'd once held a solid belief in herself as a woman who knew her own strength and worth. A single blow managed to shatter her perception of herself and others. They weren't that couple: people with dirty secrets and seedy lives. She wasn't that woman. She couldn't be.

Nauseated by the stench of burning meat, she got up and switched off the grill then snatched the wine bottle from the table. Not thinking about where she was going, she left the deck and walked around the cabin. She thought of Marty's tears and apologies, the promises he had made after hitting her. Mostly, she thought of her own eagerness to believe him.

The confrontation with Marty had sobered her. Not completely, but enough to walk a straight line down to the lake. When she reached the jetty, she flopped down and let her feet dangle as she tipped the bottle to her lips. The sky had dimmed to an ominous purple that would soon bleed into darkness. She wanted darkness.

You're a mean sloppy drunk. You liked spending my money. You couldn't get your hands on it fast enough.

She swallowed the wine wanting to erase those words from her mind, but nothing could erase the truth. Her eyes were puffy from drinking and crying, and her words had been hateful and cruel, as hateful as Marty's.

Watching the water, she spotted a duck heading towards the reeds with a line of ducklings trailing in its wake. The tiny creatures were fuzzy, downy, and newly hatched. It was early for hatchlings, probably too cold, but nature didn't always follow the rules.

The mother duck glided between the water grass. Her feathered tail flicked as she gave a low but encouraging call to her offspring. As if joined by an invisible seam that kept them steadfastly in line, the ducklings followed their mother to safety. Beth heard the fanning of wings on the air. A second later, a crow dropped out of the sky then swooped low and glided over the lake.

The last duckling in line, oblivious to the black predator above, paddled toward the reeds with its eyes fixed on its mother. Beth cried out, but it was too late. The crow snatched the duckling then soared upward, with the duckling's still paddling feet hanging from its mouth.

The crow picked up speed while the mother duck's mournful cries followed the predator as it disappeared into the trees. Dazed, Beth wasn't sure if what she'd seen was real or imagined. Outside of the mother duck's cries, there was no trace of the brutal act. The lake had returned to calm, untroubled waters.

More tears fell now for herself and the mother duck. *I like it not.* She couldn't get those words out of her head.

"Are you okay?"

The voice startled her and she let out a cry and jumped forward. Suddenly, the water sped towards her and she smelled decay and mud. The ever-present lapping of the lake grew louder as if its wet mouth wanted to pull her in and swallow her whole. A hand grabbed her shoulder and wrenched her back with enough force to leave her floundering on the jetty and blinking up at the darkening sky.

"I'm sorry. I thought you heard me coming. I didn't mean to startle you." Craig crouched beside her.

A polite dismissal formed on her lips then died just as quickly. It wasn't the look on his face that pushed her over the edge, but the gentle quality of his voice. His kindness in an unguarded, emotional moment was more than she could bear. She covered her face with her hands and sobbed.

His hands slipped under her shoulders. "Let's get you up."

Without resisting she allowed him to help her to her feet and guide her away from the water.

"It's cold out here," he said, holding her elbow. "We'll go in the office where you can warm up."

Sober up was what he meant, but was too polite to say. Craig was right about the cold, though. As they made their way across the grass, her teeth chattered.

A few minutes later, she sat not in the office but the room behind the curtain. He draped a rug around her shoulders. She clutched it under her chin.

"Better?" he asked then set down two cups of steaming tea.

Still not trusting herself to speak without dissolving into another deluge of tears, she gave a nod. They sat in silence while somewhere in the living quarters a clock ticked. Absurdly, she wondered who still owned ticking clocks.

"Can you tell me what happened?" he asked, breaking the silence. "It might help."

"It was just a stupid argument," she said. "We've been sort of going through a rough patch lately." *A rough patch.* The blandness of the words made her want to laugh but she resisted, knowing if she started, she'd cackle herself into another crying jag.

"Marty was upset, so he took off. He'll calm down and come back." There was more she could have said, so much more but she left it at that.

"Do you want me to call someone?" Craig asked.

She shook her head and wrapped her hands around the mug of hot tea. The heat felt good on her palms.

"Are you hungry? I was making toasted sandwiches."

She realised she hadn't eaten since morning. With the wine souring in her empty stomach, food seemed a good idea. She wondered why he was being so nice. Was it a sense of duty to his guests or was Craig Williams simply a kind man? Either way she was grateful to him, but couldn't help wondering what he'd say if he knew about the things she and Marty had done.

He disappeared into the kitchen. Dishes clattered and drawers opened before he returned with two plates.

They ate and sipped their drinks. The quiet was comforting and allowed some of the tension to leave her body.

"Are you still driving into Bunbury tomorrow?" she asked.

"I haven't heard from Tracy, so I'll have to go home and pick up a few things to tide me over."

Beth saw the way he looked at her. He knew what she was going to ask. Up until an hour ago her plans of leaving were only half-formed ideas that she might not have acted on. Not so any longer. The violence or threat of it had changed all that.

"Can you give me a lift?" she asked.

Chapter Eighteen

Craig offered her a key to one of the empty cabins, but she refused. Despite everything that had passed between them, Marty was still the same man she'd shared a bed with for the past five years. What difference would another night make?

It would be the last night; of that she was now sure. There was nothing Marty could say or do to change her mind. Perhaps he didn't want to change her mind. *You're a mean sloppy drunk*. Either way, her instincts told her it was safer to return to the cabin and appear remorseful.

She hesitated before heading back. Taking a glance over her shoulder to make sure Craig wasn't watching, she walked back to the lake. At the end of the jetty, the wine bottle picked up a glint of moonlight and sparkled with invitation. Sleep, dream, forget; all these things were waiting. She grabbed the bottle and as she bent, a muddy, mildewy smell hit her again and she was thankful Craig had pulled her back before she had tumbled into the lake and into the stench that reminded her of a shallow grave.

She opened the cabin door and slipped inside. Once the lights were on, she stared at the rumpled bed. It occurred to her that marriage was a secret life within a life and the bed was its heart. A marital bed could be hard or soft. Hers often felt as if it was made of glass: sometimes solid, but often fragile and brittle. For now, she still trusted that glass enough to risk one more night.

Later, after drinking the few remaining mouthfuls of wine straight from the bottle, she lay in bed. Her consciousness was in a place between sleep and wakefulness, and her thoughts weren't on the argument but on something foggier. The scratch on Marty's hand. The body wrapped in the tarp. Before her mind reached its destination, she fell asleep.

Her dreams were fragmented. The man from the rest stop with grey teeth and rheumy eyes. Lenton Hubbard wrapped, not in a tarp, but in cobwebs like a mummified meal awaiting a giant spider. Dark water filling her mouth and sucking at her limbs. Horror after horror chased her through a nightmarish landscape of endless trees.

Birdsong brought her out of sleep, blinking at the morning light coming through the windows. There were other sounds and smells. Coffee and the soft *plink* of metal on china.

Marty set a cup down on the nightstand next to the empty wine bottle then sat on the bed. His closeness forced her to pull herself up on the pillows so the two of them were at eye level.

He looked dishevelled. Dark smudges were under his eyes and he was still wearing yesterday's clothes. It was clear he'd had a rough night. A familiar sense of concern bloomed in her heart, but she resisted its pull.

"I'm sorry, pet," he said. "I can't stop thinking about what I said. I didn't mean any of it. You've got to believe that. It's just..." He rolled his shoulders. "Everything is so messed up and it got to me."

He continued talking, apologising, rationalising, justifying. She'd heard it all before, but he kept going until she couldn't stand another word.

"We both said things. We both behaved badly," she said. It was a weak response compared to his, but the best she could offer considering the circumstances.

There was gratitude in his gaze and something else that might have been admonishment, but she no longer cared enough to wonder.

"Yes," he replied, turning to her, his hazel eyes raw and puffy. "Both of us." He let those words rest for a second. "I love you. Do you love me?"

"I love you." Her response was automatic and, in some ways, heartbreakingly true.

She did love him, but the ferocity was lacking. It was an old love now. There would always be affection, but its depths had become shallowed.

"I shouldn't have grabbed you like that," he said then squeezed her leg through the bedclothes. "That's not me. You know it's not."

Beth picked up her coffee and sipped it. She made all the right noises and said all the appropriate words, wanting the conversation to end and the reconciliation to be over.

"Look." He pulled something out of his pocket and placed it on the nightstand. Her wedding ring. She looked at it with relief and sadness. One problem was solved, and another had presented itself.

"I went back," he said, his breath sour and desperate. "I searched half the night. I was starting to think it was gone for good, but then I found it." He beamed, wanting to be congratulated for his efforts.

The way he sat pinned her legs under the blankets on that side of the bed. Her mind was still fuzzy from sleep and she wished he'd get up and give her space, but there was only one way to end this saga, so she picked up the ring and slid it on her finger. It might have been her imagination, but it felt like there was grit on the inside of the band.

Marty looked satisfied. He grabbed her hand and kissed the ring.

"It's okay now," he said and, mercifully, stood. "I'm exhausted."

* * *

She waited until he was sleeping soundly on his stomach with a pillow wedged under his chin. It struck her that this was the first time she'd seen him sleep since they had arrived at the retreat. *Retreat.* The word sounded about right, but didn't quite capture the essence of the place. White Mist Lake was a place disjointed from real life, like a hideaway from the world. Picturesque, yet cold and flat, it reminded her of a tour she and Marty had once taken of Old Melbourne Gaol. The austere empty cells holding the ghosts of human misery.

Her thoughts were dramatic and blown out of proportion, fuelled by her own wretchedness. She was not so deluded as to not recognise the source of her feelings, yet understanding didn't change her dislike for White Mist Lake. But even that no longer mattered because she was leaving. The relief that came with that knowledge was swift and soothing.

Best to travel light, she decided. The house key was on Marty's key ring. Hers was at home on the kitchen bench. She fleetingly wondered how the cardboard patch job Marty had done on the window was holding up and if it had rained in Perth.

She dismissed the thought, telling herself the window was unimportant. She would only enter their home to pack what she needed and grab her car keys. The house was never really hers anyway; just a rental paid for with Marty's money – drug money, as it turned out. The window wasn't her problem, but getting the house key off the ring was.

The bunch of keys was on the nightstand on Marty's side of the bed. The ring held many keys: one for the house, the office, the mailbox, and a few others. Quentin's spare house key was there somewhere and God only knew what the others unlocked. Lifting them without waking

Marty was going to be tricky, but she hoped not impossible. *We do what we must*, as her mother was fond of saying.

She stepped carefully to the side of the bed and stood over Marty's sleeping form. Even in slumber his features were drawn with worry, yet oddly his breathing was deep and peaceful. Despite all that had happened between them, she wished she could lay her fingers on his skin and smooth away the anxiety. She even went as far as reaching out and letting her fingers hang in the air above his head. *You're a mean sloppy drunk and I'm sick of the sight of you.*

His face twitched and there was something in the pucker of his skin – something unsettling. A hint of savagery that vanished so swiftly, she was sure she'd imagined it. He was still Marty. They might have buried a body together, but he was still a decent man at heart.

It was difficult to reconcile her belief in his goodness with the fact that she felt the need to sneak away. And what about his involvement with criminals? How did decency fit in with that? She drew her hand back and focused on the keys.

Reaching for the key ring, her mind sprang back to the kitchen window covered only by a sheet of cardboard. Not even out of the cabin and she had already almost made a stupid mistake. In her mind's eye she could see their home, the narrow walkway where they stored the wheelie bins, and the side gate with a hand hole. All she had to do was reach through and pull back the latch then, just as Angel had done two nights ago, she could go through the kitchen window.

The realisation pushed her to stop and think before acting and to keep a clear head. With her temples throbbing from nights spent drinking, a clear head was easier said than done.

Marty stirred and grabbed the pillow while mumbling incoherently. The scratch on his hand looked wrinkled and red. She didn't like looking at it. *I like it not.* But why? Why did the wound bother her so? If her mind wasn't so scrambled, maybe she could work it out. Yet, even as she was cursing herself for drinking so heavily, she craved the quiet oblivion that came with the feeling of a glass in her hand. The wine was control. It allowed her to turn off the fear and unhappiness.

"Carry?"

The sound of Marty's voice startled her. Without thinking she almost answered and asked what he was carrying. Another stupid mistake narrowly avoided. Talking in his sleep was nothing new. From time to time, especially when he was stressed, he mumbled out words. Sometimes Beth replied with questions.

'Don't go where, Marty?'

'Why are you hiding?'

'Don't tell who?'

The answers were never clear and she'd never spoken of his nocturnal chatter. She wasn't sure why she had kept his sleep-talking a secret, only that the words he uttered were telling. Telling of what, she didn't know, but keeping quiet on the matter seemed prudent. She backed away from the bed. With her wallet and phone, she did her best to exit the cabin silently.

As she rushed toward the office, the promise of rain hung heavy in the sky. It was still early and with any luck they would outrun the storm.

Chapter Nineteen

"I've got a booking for next week," Craig said as soon as she entered the office. "I'm really getting the hang of this thing." He released the mouse and frowned. "No bags?"

"No bags," Beth said and jammed her hands in her coat pockets.

It seemed like Craig wanted to say more so she braced herself for questions. Instead, he only looked at her then gave a nod. Five minutes later, with the office door locked behind them, they were on the road and driving away from the retreat.

It was only after the lake disappeared behind the trees that Beth finally felt like she could breathe. The tension in her shoulders suddenly sagged and she leaned back in her seat.

"It's none of my business," Craig began.

Beth looked at him and wondered why people always stated the obvious before doing the opposite.

"But is everything okay?" he asked. "You seem sort of wired today."

She almost told him to mind his beeswax but stopped herself. He had been nothing but kind and possibly a godsend. Feeding her and rescuing her when she was stumbling around drunk and sobbing. He'd earned a few answers, or at least the right to ask a few questions without getting his head bitten off.

"The last few days have been" – she slowed down and chose her words carefully – "tense. The truth is I left while Marty was asleep." The last part came out in a rush.

Telling the truth, even if it was only a small part of it, felt good and dangerous at the same time. She suppressed a sigh of relief while waiting for Craig's reaction. In the silence she wondered if he was judging her. Was he disgusted at her cruelty, shocked that she'd run out on her sleeping husband?

Behind dark sunglasses, it was impossible to read his reaction. Why did she care what he thought? He had agreed to give her a lift. The rest was none of his business.

"Would he have tried to stop you?" Craig asked. There was no judgement in his voice, and she got the impression that he was also choosing his words carefully.

Feeling relieved, she shook her head. "More like try to talk me out of it and I'm just too tired of it all to keep going around and around."

He was interested, concerned even, but he didn't bombard her with questions. People asked so many questions not even aware that they were prying. Beth knew in the past she'd been guilty of the same ignorance, but now she had a secret to guard. Questions were the enemy.

Would it always be this way? she wondered. Would an unspoken lie hover in the corner of every conversation? Would guilt tear at her insides and gnaw into her gut, flipping and twisting until she was exhausted from the inside out?

She had no idea why she was being so honest with a stranger. The level of truth she had revealed surprised her. Apart from everything else, she *was* tired. Sick and tired of the excruciating effort of being with Marty.

She watched the forest and wished for her old life. A job she was good at and colleagues who liked her, a crappy apartment, and even the worry of opening a bill she wasn't sure she could afford to pay. And Ethan. The minutia of her old life – dull and sometimes laborious – now seemed uncomplicated and safe. It was difficult to remember why she'd been so eager to give it up.

"I just need time to think, if that makes any sense," she said then looked at her hands and caught sight of her wedding ring.

Where did Marty find it? she wondered, visualising the burial site and the arc of old trees that stood tall and gnarled over the body. Had the ring been in the dirt of the grave?

"Makes sense," Craig replied.

She wasn't sure if he was just being polite, but he was easy to talk to and a calming presence. A refreshing change from the tension of her relationship and the underlying uncertainty of the past few days. She glanced in his direction and couldn't help smiling. The granddad jumper he wore was so at odds with Marty's trendy garb.

"You've been raiding your father's wardrobe again," she said trying to lighten the mood.

He laughed. "I grabbed it this morning. It's clean, but don't come too close or you'll choke on the smell of mothballs from—"

He stopped talking and focused his attention on the rear-view mirror. Beth turned in her seat with her body tensed and her chest tight. The Mazda sped toward them, closing the gap at breakneck speed.

"It's Marty," she gasped. "I don't know how he knew."

She laced her fingers into her hair then squeezed her temples. What now? Why couldn't he just let her go? Her thoughts piled up one on top of the other as the Mazda pulled closer and drove on the wrong side of the road. After catching a glimpse of his determined face, she realised he would never let her go. Without warning, Marty pulled in behind them.

Glancing over her shoulder, she saw the Mazda's grille growing larger as it bore down on Craig's sister's little Hyundai.

"Jesus, what does he think he's doing?" Craig asked, gripping the wheel tighter.

"Pull over," Beth demanded, knowing there was no other way. She'd been crazy to think otherwise and that lapse in judgement had dragged Craig into the chaos.

"I don't think that's a good idea, Beth. What if—"

"Please," she insisted. "Just stop."

Craig continued to drive. "Maybe we should keep going, at least until we get to the shops."

"Just pull over!" Beth shrieked a little too loudly.

Craig looked surprised, but to her relief he flicked on the indicator and reduced his speed.

"Stay in the car," she said once they came to a stop.

"This isn't a good idea," Craig said, turning in his seat and watching as Marty flung the driver's door open and jumped out. "He was driving like a maniac."

Beth grabbed Craig's arm. Apart from when he saved her from tumbling into the lake, it was the first time she had touched him and the action of it felt too familiar.

"He's fine." She lightened her tone. "Trust me. He's just being dramatic."

She couldn't say why, but it felt important for Craig to stay in the car. "Trust me," she repeated and got out.

Marty made no move to approach as Beth walked toward him. She noticed his hands were hooked on his hips and there was something menacing in the way his feet were planted.

In the seconds it took her to reach him, she formulated a story and the best way to handle the situation. It occurred to her that handling Marty had become a way of life – a full-time job.

"Why did you get up? You said you were exhausted," she said before he could speak.

There was uncertainty in his expression. This clearly wasn't what he'd been expecting.

"Where are you going, Beth?" His mouth was tight, but he looked unsure of himself.

"Craig's giving me a lift to the shops." She grimaced. "I need something to eat that doesn't come out of a vending machine."

Marty watched her unconvinced.

She dropped her voice. "Okay. I wanted a bottle of wine and I knew you'd give me a hard time about it."

His hands dropped to his sides, making him look defeated. She saw blondish-red stubble on his chin, not the carefully cultivated growth he usually sported but an unkempt rasp that made him look haggard.

"Jesus, Beth. If you wanted wine that badly, I would have gone and bought it for you. I told you I didn't mean any of that stuff I said last night."

That badly. The words stung and she found herself struggling to ignore them. "I know, but what's the big deal? You went off while I was in bed yesterday. I *can* do things for myself." Her voice sounded stronger, wounded. "I'm not helpless, you know?"

He glanced over her shoulder. "Who's he?"

She followed his gaze to where Craig sat waiting in the car.

"Just the maintenance man." She made a tutting sound. "Well, you're here now. You might as well drive me to the shops. I'll go and tell him there's been a change of plan."

Marty grabbed her wrist and squeezed, but quickly loosened his grip then lifted her hand and rubbed her wedding ring with his thumb. While watching him, she noticed the scratch on his hand again. There was something startling about the look of it. Suddenly, she didn't see Marty but the tarp flapping open and exposing Lenton's face. She saw blood and gore. With the sickening memory came a swift realisation and the connection she'd been trying to make. It all came together, and the weight of it made her almost stagger.

She pulled her hand away unable to tolerate his touch. The cold she barely noticed a second ago now travelled up her legs and spread like a cancer.

"I'll be right back," she said through dry lips.

Walking felt strange. Her legs were like frozen petrified sticks that made her movements seem stilted. She could feel Marty's gaze on her back so she did her best to walk naturally. At the same time, she wanted to run. She could see herself jumping in the car next to Craig and screaming for him to drive.

"All okay?" Craig asked when she stood at the driver's window.

"Yes, all good." She gave a shrug of embarrassment. "Sorry for all this, but I guess I overreacted. It wouldn't be the first time. Marty's really eaten up over the argument so I'm going with him. We're going to grab some lunch and talk things over. Patch things up."

The icy sensation had reached her chest and made speaking difficult.

"Okay," Craig said then glanced back to where Marty was standing beside the Mazda. "Are you sure?"

Beth did her best to give a convincing nod while she silently willed Craig to wind up his window and get the hell away from this lonely stretch of road, because she had the distinct impression that her charming, sometimes easy-going husband was extremely dangerous.

"I'll go," he said. "But first give me your phone."

He held out his hand clearly determined. Turning her back so Marty wouldn't see the exchange, she handed the phone over. For someone who knew little about computers, his fingers worked deftly over the mobile's screen.

"Okay." He handed it back. "Call me if you need anything. And you better juice that up." He nodded at the phone. "It's about to die on you."

Chapter Twenty

"Why didn't you take the car?" Marty asked as they drove toward the shops. "Why take a lift from a stranger when we have a car? Sometimes I wonder about you, Beth."

Why did you lie to me, Beth? That's what he was really asking.

"The keys were right next to your head and I didn't want to jingle them and wake you." It was the truth. The best lies were built on the truth. She had learned that from him.

The shop turned out to be a hybrid, a mix of roadhouse and mini supermarket. Vine. A trendy name for a holidaymaker's pit stop. They grabbed avocado and salad sandwich wraps, a bag of locally grown macadamias, wine, and a few other bits and pieces.

Feigning interest in reading labels, she wasted time tossing things in their basket. All the while she scanned the store looking for the bathrooms. As they were passing the fridges, she saw a rustic iron plaque hanging over a side door that said 'Toilets'.

"I need the bathroom," she said. "I won't be long."

He fixed her with those hazel eyes and under the shop's harsh lights his irises looked almost red.

She moved quickly, not giving him time to question or delay her. If she hesitated, her resolve would fracture and she wouldn't have the strength later. But more than that, she wanted to be away from those bizarre red eyes. It was like she could feel them burning her skin.

Once she flung the door open, she found herself outside. The toilets were housed in a separate structure that had entrances on either side. The doors were marked 'Sheilas' and 'Blokes'. Someone's idea of hilarity. Under different circumstances she would have giggled and asked Marty to take her photo under the 'Sheilas' sign. She thought of the caption she would write when she posted the picture on Instagram: *The eighties called. They want their sign back.* It was a stupid thought, one to distract her from what she was about to do.

Running, she crossed the ground between the buildings and dove through the bathroom door. After almost colliding with a young woman carrying a toddler, she stepped aside and mumbled an apology as the woman tutted and brushed past her.

The bathroom reminded her of the cabin, all wooden walls and mirrors with chunky frames. Her tongue felt dry so she lunged for the basin. Using her hand, she scooped deliciously cold water into her mouth then splashed some on her cheeks.

What was she doing wasting time faffing around with water when Marty was undoubtedly wondering what was taking her so long? He was probably on his way to the toilet block at that moment and knowing him he would walk straight into the ladies'. That sort of thing wouldn't stop him, not Marty Jacobsen, the man who always had a plan.

With a fugitive glance at the door, she dashed into one of the empty stalls, closed and latched the door, then pulled out her mobile. One swipe and the screen came to life and just as quickly died. Staring open-mouthed at the useless device, she felt something hot boiling up inside her.

The taste of it flooded her mouth, making her scowl and shudder.

She wanted to smash the mobile. Instead, she slammed the phone's screen against her forehead and was pleased with the *whap* sound it made when it hit her skin. The pleasure was fleeting and quickly replaced by pain.

The ridiculousness of her actions almost turned her anger into self-pity.

She flipped the toilet lid down and sat. Was she angry or terrified? Both? Was it possible to be both? Hot and cold. Salt and oranges. Once again, her thoughts were swamped by seesawing emotions.

"You okay in here, pet?"

Marty's voice worked on her like a gunshot. She jumped to her feet, then froze. What now? If the phone had worked, she'd be stalling him until the police arrived or going with him expecting sirens to meet them at the retreat. Without help, was she just supposed to get back in the car and pretend everything was fine? Could she do that?

"Beth?" He was inside the restroom. She could hear his footsteps approaching. "Are you in here, pet?"

For one insane moment she considered not answering. Instead, she would cower and pray until he gave up and went away. She should have run and hid in the bush or behind a parked car while she had the chance. She'd had the perfect opportunity, but now it was too late.

"Jesus, Marty. Can't you give me a minute to use the toilet?" She stabbed at the flush to prove her point.

"I'm worried about you, Beth." His voice was close now, on the other side of the door. "The way you've been acting scares me."

Beth swallowed. Her throat was still dry. "My stomach's all over the place. Can you please wait outside before someone comes in, sees you and calls the manager?" Her churning emotions gave her voice the perfect note of exasperation.

"Whatever you want, pet." He sounded contrite, but his tone was a little too stiff to be believable.

Beth doubted she would ever believe another word that came out of his mouth.

* * *

"What is it?" Marty asked.

They were driving toward the retreat with pop music filling the car. Something upbeat and catchy, but she couldn't think of the name of the song. She was usually good with that sort of thing. Song names, singers, films – she knew them all, but not today. All she could think about was that dreadful moment when Marty's scratch stood out against the blue colour of his shirt. Just like Lenton's bloody face against the blue tarp.

"Why must there be something?" she asked in a voice just above the music.

"It's too loud," he said and reached for the dial.

"No, I like it," she insisted even though she had no idea what they were listening to. Anything was better than silence or banal conversation.

"That's better," he replied, ignoring her request and turning the music off completely.

"Something's wrong. You're not yourself," he said. "We can't get through this if you won't talk to me."

She didn't answer. She couldn't trust herself not to say too much. Instead, she stared out the window with one arm braced on the door. For some reason, the drive felt painfully long going back. And the questions kept coming.

"What did you tell that maintenance man?" he asked.

"I didn't tell him anything." Beth didn't dare meet his gaze. "He needed help with the computer in the office and I asked for a lift to the shops."

"What do you know about him?"

She thought for a moment. It seemed a strange question, like something out of a television show. Did Marty get all of his ideas from the TV?

"Not much," she replied. "His sister runs the place, but she's taken off for a few days. You know, the woman who checked you in the other night?"

Marty shifted in his seat but didn't say anything. Hopefully, he was satisfied with her scant knowledge of the maintenance man.

They turned onto the road that led to the lake. A few seconds later, the water emerged between the trees. It was as though the lake had been waiting for her, mocking her attempt to leave it behind.

Once they were in the cabin, Marty busied himself unloading their purchases while Beth retrieved her phone charger and set her mobile to charge in the bathroom.

They sat on the back deck where the smell of burnt meat still lingered, only there was a new odour. The cheesy and rotten stench of dead ants. She stared at the sandwich wrap purchased from the shop with the quirky name, then broke off a bit of pita and put it in her mouth while watching Marty wolf his food down. It occurred to her that he always ate like a greedy child.

"You should clean that barbeque," she said. "The meat is attracting ants."

He jumped to his feet and turned to stare at the grill. Swearing under his breath, he rushed inside and returned with a plastic bag. Tutting and grimacing, he used the bag like a glove to pick up the charred meat and to swat at the ants. Entomophobia. She once looked the word up. It meant a fear of insects. Drawing his attention to the bugs was cruel and petty, but she enjoyed watching him squirm. As he wrestled the steak into the bag, he looked like he was handling a deadly snake. He'd been less squeamish about the dead body. Her anger resurfaced.

"These fucking ants are driving me insane," he muttered. Beth thought he wasn't exaggerating because he really did look unhinged.

Suddenly, tears were in her eyes and she realised she was crying. With her mouth stuffed with pita, she wiped her cheeks on her sleeve while his back was still to her.

"There," he said then sat down again. "That's one more thing done."

One more thing crossed off Marty's list. The anger bit at her as if the ants were on her skin instead of crawling across the deck. *That's one more thing done.* She imagined him standing over Lenton and saying those words.

"You killed that man," she said, not as a question, but as a statement that she hadn't known she was going to make.

Saying the words aloud hadn't been her intention, but they were in her mind and, like her tears, they just leaked out.

Marty sat still, seemingly caught between surprise and fear, or was it anger? Why couldn't she read her own husband's expression?

"It's true." The words made her sick and yet she asked. "Isn't it?"

"What are you talking about?" he said with an indulgent chuckle.

It was a chuckle she knew very well. *Beth, you're being over-dramatic. Beth, you're being an alarmist.* It was his you're-too-cute-to-be-taken-seriously laugh.

She held his gaze and the laughter dried up.

"Beth," – he spoke with caution – "I know things have been stressful for you and that's my fault. All of it. I should have seen this coming, but after everything it's not surprising" – he ran a hand over his chin and she heard the rasp of stubble – "you've got it all mixed up in your mind. The violence and the body. You're not thinking straight. Your wild imagination is driving you crazy."

He made it all sound so plausible and so rational that she felt herself being reeled in. While his version implied she was having a nervous breakdown, it *was* more attractive than the alternative.

"When the tarp fell open, I saw his head," she said. "There was blood and bone." Her voice had risen, but she couldn't stop. "You said Angel bit him on the thigh and he bled out."

"He did," Marty insisted. "You're just—"

"Then why was that man's head bashed in?" Beth narrowed her eyes. "I saw it and even then, I was too sickened to take it in – too blind and stupid to understand."

A bird squawked from a tree startled by the shrillness of her voice.

"*Shh!*" Marty hissed then glanced around. "Keep your voice down."

"I won't keep my voice down." She pushed back her chair and stood over him. "How could you? All this time we've been cooking barbeque, going for walks, and having sex." She waved a hand at the cabin. "How could you do something so disgusting?"

He stood and grabbed her under the arm. "Shut up and get inside." He shoved her toward the door, opened it, then pushed her inside.

Chapter Twenty-one

Somehow, she regained her balance. Marty's shove had propelled her almost to the bed and in the process of steadying herself she had whacked her knee on the nightstand.

Grabbing her leg, she limped half a meter and flopped onto the unmade bed. Marty loomed over her, his eyes wide and glassy. Her body tensed in readiness for a blow.

She had gone too far and had pushed him over the edge. Fuelled by anger and outrage, she had stupidly discarded the fact that they were alone at White Mist Lake and that the only other resident, Craig, was kilometres away.

Marty made no move to hurt her. To her surprise, he fell to his knees sobbing. With his face in his hands, his shoulders shook.

"I'm sorry, so sorry," he moaned. "I keep trying to turn things around and find a way out. But... But I just keep losing myself."

Uncovering his face, he touched her knee then gently ran his fingers over it. "Did I hurt you? I didn't mean to be so rough. You're all right, aren't you? Oh, Beth. I'm sorry."

His face was red and wet with tears. She'd never seen him like this – so vulnerable. Despite everything he'd done she couldn't bare his pain.

Reluctantly, she placed her hands on his head. "I'm fine. It's nothing. I just bumped my knee. Don't cry."

Marty continued to sob, this time with his head in her lap, murmuring her name as though it was some sort of magical incantation that would make everything better. He was like a frightened child seeking comfort. As always, she gave him what he needed by stroking his hair and whispering platitudes. He gripped her sides in a way that was both frantic and pathetic. His despair was almost worse than his anger and his sobs pulled at her heart.

Before she spoke, she promised herself she'd walk on eggshells because Marty was fragile, and fragile people were apt to break.

"This has gone too far," she said when he finally quieted down. "We're out of our depth, Marty. Surely, you see that?"

Sitting back on his knees, he pulled up his shirt and scrubbed his face. "I didn't mean to do *anything*. It just happened." His eyes were imploring. "You'll see, pet. If you just let me tell you, you'll understand."

She nodded for him to continue, unsure that she'd ever understand how Lenton Hubbard's head came to be bashed in on their kitchen floor.

"After you left to take the dog to the vet, I was sweeping up the glass," he began, while settling himself on the rug with his legs crossed. The sobbing had ceased, and he looked like a man getting ready to share a fascinating story.

"I heard a noise on the far side of the bench and that's when I saw him. His leg was torn up just like I told you. There was a lot of blood. A pool of the stuff. I realised what I'd heard was skidding. He was trying to sit up and his hand kept slipping on the blood."

Beth remembered how much blood had been on the floor and the smell of it, the way the mop slid over the thick liquid, and Marty's rapid movements while blotting up the gore and then dumping it into the bucket. She recalled watching as Marty had emptied the bloody water into the sink. And, she'd wondered, how he was able to remain so impassive while she had to bite on her sleeve to stop herself from screaming.

"He still had the knife in his hand. That's why he couldn't get purchase," Marty explained. "He saw me and said something. I don't remember what exactly – something about killing me. If I let that happen, if he got up, I knew he'd stab me and then when you got back, he would have been waiting. I couldn't let him hurt you. I *had* to stop him. I did what I had to do."

His words started coming out in a rush. "He came into our home – our home, Beth." He slammed his fist on his knee. "Attacked you in my house. *My* house. I had to put a stop to it."

She gripped the sheets to stop herself from springing off the bed and running. She didn't want to hear the rest, but she had set the confession in motion. If she'd just kept her mouth shut, she wouldn't be sitting on the bed listening to this nightmarish story. And it was a story, of that she was sure. At the same time she became aware of how quickly she had come to doubt every word that came out of his mouth.

"I grabbed something from the drawer and hit him. It was quick," he said as if that made what he'd done excusable. "So quick it was a blur. I barely remember doing it. I just acted and I'm not sorry. I did what I had to, to protect you. To protect us!"

"What did you grab?" Beth asked.

He looked confused and his eyes were dry. She saw no sign of tears.

"You said you grabbed something from the drawer and hit him. What did you grab?" she repeated. She worried that his temper might flare, but she'd come too far to stop now. She had to know.

His expression altered. A shift so slight it was almost imperceptible. He was thinking and trying to decide how much to reveal, trying to see beyond the question and read her intention.

"The steak mallet. I reached into the drawer and just grabbed something. Don't worry. It's gone. I wrapped it up with him." He held his hands out to her with his palms up. "You see? I had no choice, but it's taken care of. We're safe."

"Why the lies?" she asked. "You keep telling me how much you need me, but you tell me half-truths. You keep me in the dark and then try to make me feel like I'm going crazy."

He got to his feet then closed the space between them by sitting on the bed.

"I couldn't tell you, not when I could see what all this was doing to you. I wanted to spare you the added horror." He slipped his arm around her. "I didn't want to hurt you any more than I already had. I didn't want you to think less of me."

Beth almost laughed. It would have been funny if it hadn't been so frightening. One of them had lost their mind but she wasn't sure which. Maybe they had both gone completely mad.

"Marty." She shrugged off his arm and turned a little to face him. "I want to go home."

Trance-like, he got up and went into the bathroom. It seemed as if he'd forgotten she was there. She heard water running and splashing. Perhaps he was too overwhelmed to answer her. If she persisted or nagged him, things might blow up. No, not things, she told herself. Marty might blow up.

He was a murderer. She had to keep that in mind now. That knowledge always had to stay at the forefront of her mind. The idea of him wielding the steak mallet was too gruesome to contemplate, yet her imagination was intent on conjuring up the scene. *That's one more thing done.* Had he said those words while holding the mallet just like he had ten minutes ago when he cleaned the barbeque?

I can't live like this. The realisation leapt into her mind. How could she be expected to sleep with him or sit across the dinner table and look into those watchful eyes? How could she talk to her mother or sister while keeping this dreadful secret locked in her throat like a hunk of bone that wanted to be spewed out?

He would go to prison. Putting him behind bars would be her burden to carry. Not for life, though. There were mitigating circumstances so perhaps he'd receive a lenient sentence. She would go back to work. Good hairdressers were always in demand and she could use her maiden name, Rowe. It was a good name. She had liked being Elizabeth Rowe.

The water was still running when she got up and began packing. With a pair of socks in hand, she froze. What if Marty had been telling the truth? If he hadn't stopped Lenton, he could have killed Marty. Lenton could have butchered her the minute she walked through the front door. If the situation had been reversed, would Lenton Hubbard waste time worrying about their deaths? Would he turn himself in to the police? No. Men like Hubbard and Pike didn't give a damn about human life, so why was she letting his murder tear her apart?

But Marty had blamed it on Angel, a childish voice inside her spoke up. Marty had never liked Angel and always complained that Angel was too big and too much trouble. How many times had Marty asked why she hadn't chosen a little fluffy thing? She would usually laugh off the question or say something glib like, *He chose me.* She would say it with just enough humour to disguise the depth of her words.

Marty had agreed to a puppy, something small and easy to manage. That had been the great compromise. *Her* compromise. But she'd given up motherhood so shouldn't the choice of dog have been hers to make? Instead of going to a breeder, she had driven to the pound with the windows down and her hair billowing around her.

Seven-month-old Angel sat in a cage with a handful of other young dogs. None of them were purebreds or trendy mixes, only mutts that were almost past the cute stage. Amongst the wild excitement of the other dogs, Angel, the largest puppy Beth had ever seen, sat unmoving against the back of the cage. His honey-coloured eyes were wary and fearful.

'Hello,' she'd said.

His head cocked at the sound of her voice and he came closer.

Maybe he *did* choose her because in that moment it seemed he'd been waiting for her and instantly recognised her voice. After he neared the wire, she crouched so they were at eye level.

'You're a little angel,' she'd said and his sweet ears, previously flattened with fear, had pricked up. The wariness disappeared and he smiled.

She knew Marty believed she had brought Angel home to prove some childish point. *You said I could have a dog so I got the one I knew you'd hate.* But that hadn't been the case. It had never been the reason. There was something in Angel's eyes that she had desperately needed. Love? Devotion? Protection? Maybe all of those things. All the things Marty couldn't give her.

Thinking about Angel, her resolve weakened. If she went to the police, surely she'd be arrested. After all, she had helped a murderer dispose of a body. No one would believe she hadn't known that Marty had killed Lenton Hubbard. Why would they, when she could barely believe her own stupidity?

The socks dropped in the suitcase. Once they were home, things would be clearer. She'd be able to settle on a course of action. If not the police, then divorce. A new life.

"What are you doing?" Marty asked from the bathroom doorway.

His hair was damp and combed into its usual style and his shirt was untucked.

"I'm packing," she said then looked around to see if she was leaving anything behind. "I told you I want to go home."

"And we will," he said. "First thing tomorrow."

Beth felt the strength leaking out of her. Maybe her prison sentence had already begun.

"I need your help," he said. "This one last thing and then we'll leave."

Chapter Twenty-two

"This can't be happening." She sat on the floor with no idea how she had ended up there. "It just keeps getting worse."

Marty stood at the window, fiddling with the curtains. Sunlight touched her skin and she turned her face to meet its warmth. Somewhere out there was light and laughter and people going about their lives without a care in the world. A few days ago, she'd been one of those people, but now it seemed like a dream.

"I want you out of the way when he gets here," Marty said over his shoulder. "You can ask that maintenance bloke for another cabin. Tell him we had a fight and you want to be on your own. I bet he'll be more than happy to help. Beth?"

He turned and appeared confused to see her on the floor. "Are you listening?"

The mild heat made her feel pleasantly sluggish – sleepy. As she crawled toward the bed then climbed in, she was aware of Marty's voice. She felt empty, scraped dry of emotion, like a shell with nothing left and only an echo of her old self.

The last thing she heard before falling asleep was, "I'll give it to him and that will be it."

She experienced a moment of confusion and briefly wondered who was being given what, but the thoughts were cut off as her mind sought then found comfort in sleep.

* * *

It was late afternoon when she woke and it occurred to her that she'd been sleeping, drinking, and crying too much. She had developed a whole new way of life where it was easier to drink, cry, and sleep rather than face reality.

The cabin was quiet. The air always felt lighter whenever Marty wasn't around. She should have been taking the opportunity to move, to do something. *Act now!* her mind screamed.

As she stood, she pulled a blanket off the bed and wrapped it around her shoulders. She couldn't seem to get warm. Cocooned in the blanket, she hobbled into the bathroom vaguely aware of the pain in her knee. Her phone was gone. She stared at the socket and trailing cord while blinking in disbelief. How could her phone be gone? Had she forgotten where she'd put it?

Her knee, the phone, her life; it was all a blur. Shivering, she turned to the kitchenette. Efficient as always, Marty had put the wine in the mini fridge to chill. *Yes, he's a killer*, she imagined herself saying from the witness stand. *But he's efficient around the house.*

"Thank you, pet," she said, grabbing the bottle.

Just a small glass to take the edge off. A splash of wine and then she'd be able to calm down and think.

With a glass in her hand and still swaddled in the blanket, she moved to the window. Marty was standing on the jetty. At the sight of him, she experienced a flash of hatred as sudden and as cold as the waters of the lake. She wasn't sure if it was the wine or the hate, but she felt light-headed.

When did this all start? she wondered, because it certainly wasn't three nights ago. But surely it wasn't possible to go from love to hate so nimbly. *Orange to salt.* Emotions at the extreme end of the spectrum and neither were reliable.

She still felt dizzy, yet for the first time in a long while she saw her life with clarity, not only the drug money and the break-in, but her marriage. No. More than her marriage because it had started before the wedding.

Marty had splashed cash and insisted on paying for everything. A huge diamond engagement ring. Urging her to buy the most expensive dress. Encouraging her to quit work so he could give her everything and take care of her. Surprising her with tickets to New Zealand for their honeymoon. The minute the plans were laid and all of the lavish arrangements paid for, he had sprung the no-child clause.

Bitter arguments followed, cruel words and periods of silence. Then two months after the wedding, Marty's mood swings became apparent. Dark weeks followed by excited planning and dizzying displays of affection and extravagant gifts. By the time they celebrated their first wedding anniversary, he had hit her for the first time.

There were nights when she was unable to sleep and would lie awake in the wee hours with crazy thoughts running through her mind. The wee hours became a conduit for crazy thoughts. Memories of all the childbirth stories she'd heard while styling clients' hair. Horror stories women told while flipping casually through magazines or as they kept a critical eye on the scissors. How funny it was that women could recount the worst pain of their lives with such ease. Every time they described their pain, it had sent a cold finger of dread up her spine.

Yet in those early hours when she couldn't sleep, she found herself longing for that pain. That pain was her right. A right he had stolen and, God, did she hate him for it. So, perhaps the break-in and murder merely pulled the whole sorry mess into the light. In hindsight, it had been the murder that broke the camel's back.

There'd been problems from the beginning, but nothing compared to what they were going through now. Over the last few days, she had watched the layers peel back. Everything she thought she knew had slipped away. Was Marty losing himself or revealing himself? Which truth was more terrifying?

What would he say if he came back and caught her drinking before the sun was down? What could he say? *You're a drunk?* Murderer trumped drunk. *Murder.* The word kept coming back. She hoped the wine would keep the word at bay, but every time it came into her mind, the force of the shock hit with renewed strength.

His teary confession and her obediently comforting him; she *was* a good pet. No wonder he liked to keep her close. She finished the glass and returned to the fridge for a refill. Mid pour, she heard an engine and rushed to the window. Unable to see the road, she opened the door and peered out like a frightened child.

She was so relieved to see Craig's little red car that she dropped the blanket and ran. Glancing to her right, she saw Marty, who was still on the jetty, turn to watch her. She wondered if the sun reflecting off the lake had turned his eyes that strange reddish colour again. Her knee ached and she was aware of his gaze, but she kept running.

Craig parked around the side of the office. As he climbed out, he did a double take when he saw her barrelling toward him. She saw his mouth open in surprise and then the world slowed.

Unexpectedly, her hurt knee wobbled then folded under her. The sky came into view. Someone called her name as she landed on her back with a bone-jarring thump.

Craig's face appeared above her. His lips were moving, but she couldn't keep track of the words. He lifted her and she was struck by the ease at which he handled her weight.

Half walking but leaning heavily on him, she allowed him to lead her to the office. As he fumbled with the keys, she realised she was clutching his jacket like a fragile old woman and forced her fingers to unlock. After the door opened, she walked inside on unsteady legs.

"Come on," he said then led her around the counter and into the back room. "Let's sit you down and get you warmed up. You're freezing."

He was kind and gentle; everything that Marty wasn't and hadn't been for a long time. Craig wrapped a rug around her shoulders and turned on an ancient gas heater. She wondered if he was getting sick of always having to warm her up.

A few moments later he pressed a cup into her hand. "I've put in some sugar. It's supposed to help."

She mumbled her thanks as he sat in an armchair. She could imagine what she looked like through Craig's eyes: her hair plastered to her head, her clothes rumpled from sleep, eyes puffy, and the stink of wine on her breath. She felt repulsed by the thought and could only cringe at what he saw. But he was being nice – too nice to let it show on his face. No doubt he regretted those first friendly conversations because now he probably felt stuck with her.

"I'm sorry to be such a pain," she said and took a sip of the overly sweet tea. "It's just that I need…" I need to tell you the truth, she thought and could feel the story bubbling up in her throat. Swallowing, she continued. "I need another cabin for the night. Somewhere quiet where I can think. You can put it on our credit card," she finished in a whisper.

He didn't speak right away. Was he trying to think of a polite way to ask her and Marty to leave? She wouldn't blame him, not with all their drama. Nothing was more excruciating than being dragged into a couple's marital turmoil. He should be running for the hills, but she desperately hoped that he'd continue being kind. God knew she needed it.

"Of course. No problem. I'll put you in cabin two. It'll give you a bit of a buffer zone." The last words had come out awkwardly.

He got up and disappeared into the office. While he was gone, she took a few more sips of tea. Craig was right. The sugar did help. Well, sort of.

He returned with the key. Instead of going to the armchair, he pushed back the coffee table and crouched in front of her. Unsure what he meant to do, she pulled back.

He stared into her eyes, and she was struck by how attractive he looked, wearing more age-appropriate clothing. His deep tan suggested time outdoors and she wondered if he was a surfer. She almost winced at the absurdity of the thought. This was one of the worst days of her life and over the last week there had been some stiff competition for that title. Yet here she was, marvelling at this kind man's looks.

It had to be the shock. She was exhausted and not thinking clearly so her mind was trying to latch onto anything that would distract her from the fact that Marty was a murderer.

"Has something happened?" Craig asked. "If you need help, I'll drive you out of here right now."

She could smell his aftershave, sharp and clean. She wanted to let him help so badly that it almost hurt.

He touched her hand and she looked down at his fingers. His jacket had ridden up revealing a bandage on his forearm. He was still talking, but she couldn't drag her eyes away from the dressing. Spots of blood had formed a semicircle. A bite? A dog bite?

Afraid to lift her head, she asked, "What happened to your arm?"

"That?" he asked then pulled the sleeve down to cover the bandage. "I caught it when I was fixing that leak in cabin two."

"I thought you said you fixed the taps in cabin three?" she said, aware that her voice sounded strangled because the smell of his aftershave had invaded her throat.

"Did I say two? I meant cabin three." He held out the key. "Are you sure you don't want me to drive you into Bunbury?"

While setting the cup on the table, she spilled half its contents. Being careful not to touch his fingers, she took the key. The way he crouched blocked her from standing so she waited until he got out of her way.

"Sorry about the spill," she said as she jumped to her feet and rushed toward the front of the building.

"Wait," he called. She heard him behind her and was sure he was coming after her.

She didn't stop, but by the time she reached the office door, he had caught up to her and put his hand on the glass to bar her from opening it.

"I'll walk you to your cabin," he said as he towered over her from behind. "It might be safer."

She kept her hand on the door handle and didn't look back at him. "No," she said too loudly. "I mean, there's no need. You've done enough."

"Are you sure?" he insisted.

"Really. You've been a great help, but I just want to be alone, so…" She waited and wondered if he could hear her heart hammering.

Getting the message, he let go of the door and stepped back. As soon as he was out of the way, she tore the door open and rushed out.

"But if you need anything!" he called.

Whatever else he had to say was lost to the wind as she bounded across the car park toward cabin two. She didn't waste time checking to see if Marty was still watching.

It took a few attempts to get the key in the lock, but once she did, she pushed the door with so much force that she fell into the cabin and landed on her hands and knees. Scrambling onto her feet, she slammed the door and locked it. Clutching the key, it occurred to her that Craig might have a spare. Panicked, she pulled a chair from against the wall and jammed it under the doorknob.

Panting, she bent forward and put her hands on her knees. It looked like a bite and his reaction seemed odd. Those blue eyes and the aftershave. Why hadn't she noticed them before? Was she over-reacting and jumping to conclusions? What about the missing sister?

She turned in a circle and spotted the back door. It was the same as the one in cabin ten. She checked the lock then looked for something to use as a barricade. With nothing else for her to use, she dragged the nightstand sideways and propped it under the handle. It wasn't much, but at least Craig would make a hell of a racket if he tried to get in.

Chapter Twenty-three

Was Craig Joe Pike? Beth sat on the bed and thought back to the night she and Marty arrived. Tracy had checked Marty in. Joe Pike could have followed them from Perth then gotten rid of Tracy and set himself up as Craig. She shivered at the idea of Tracy looking up from the computer and smiling as Joe Pike entered the office.

It was coming together in her mind and while the notion terrified her, it made sense – almost. But wouldn't Marty have recognised Joe? Thinking back to the day when Marty nearly ran her and Craig off the road, she told Craig to stay in the car. As she recalled, Craig didn't put up much of a fuss. He could have ignored her instruction and stepped out of the vehicle at any time, but he didn't.

When Marty parked behind them, there would have been no way he could have recognised Craig as Pike because Craig had his back to Marty. Even today when she ran across the parking lot while Marty watched from the jetty, the sun would have been in his eyes and the distance would have stopped him from seeing Craig clearly.

She wrapped her arms around herself. It seemed plausible that Marty had no idea that Joe Pike had been at White Mist Lake these past two days. It made perfect sense and no sense at all. Why would Pike hang around and play games? If he wanted to finish what he had started in Perth, why wait?

"Because he's a sadistic maniac," she said through clenched teeth.

The story about Tracy could have been fabricated. For all Beth knew, Tracy didn't have a brother. Who's to say that Pike didn't kill Tracy and come up with the whole saga about a sister who was apt to go missing? Even his clothes had been off. If Marty hadn't almost run them off the road, who knew where Craig would have taken her? She didn't want to imagine what he might have done once he had her alone and somewhere isolated.

Without thinking, her gaze darted between the two doors. There was also Marty to consider, especially after he announced his latest plan. A plan he hadn't mentioned until *after* he confessed to bashing a man's head in with a steak mallet. No wonder she had crawled into bed and curled into the foetal position instead of paying attention.

Her eyes landed on a complimentary bottle of red wine. It sat on top of the mini fridge tied with red ribbon just like the one in cabin ten. The ribbon made her think of Tracy's cherry-red blouse and how a small piece of the fabric had wound up caught in a bush.

Did it all mean something or was her overwrought mind making connections that weren't there? Was it possible that Craig really did hurt his arm while fixing a tap, and that his aftershave just happened to smell similar to the one Joe Pike had worn?

"I like it not," she whispered, barely aware that she had spoken.

Her instincts told her to pull the chair away from the door and run to Marty, but those were old instincts. The instincts of three days ago. Now she couldn't be sure if she'd be any safer with Marty than with Pike.

Going to the window, she looked out over the retreat. Cabin two had a better view of the office and because of the positioning of the huts, she could also see cabin ten. It would be dark soon. Which way was safe?

She turned from the window and to the wine. It would be nice to sleep again, to drift away and wake when it was all over.

What was it Marty said as she fell asleep that afternoon? *I'll give it to him and that will be it.* She mouthed the words – Marty's words.

A memory surfaced and she tried to grasp it. She had to try and figure out exactly what Marty had planned for tonight. But sweet oblivion called to her, telling her to leave Marty and Joe Pike to their fate. Let them kill each other for all she cared. She was leaving in the morning even if she had to walk all the way to Bunbury.

Time passed, maybe half an hour, and she found herself sitting on the floor, staring at the wine. Her thoughts had slipped back to the night of the break-in when she'd been forced inside their bedroom to where Marty sat slumped with that helpless look on his face. Only this time she considered his expression with a sharper eye. It wasn't fear or helplessness, not even acceptance. What Beth saw was indifference, a look that told Pike to do what he must.

The memory shook her. Was that what she saw or was her mind inserting details to support her newborn hatred? Amidst all the panic and fear, could she be sure of anything from that night? The answer seemed to be yes. After everything she'd seen and heard from Marty over the past few days, she had no trouble believing he would consider Joe Pike's attack on her as collateral damage.

She imagined Marty buying her flowers and a piece of jewellery or perhaps even arranging a trip to Paris. In his mind, making things up to her would be a simple matter of finding the price, like an equation that he could solve with money. Beth had been brutalised so compensation was in order. And why not? She'd given up motherhood for not much more.

The intruders came for their pound of flesh and Marty had been prepared to watch them take it without so much as a struggle. In her mind's eye, she saw herself half-naked and sobbing; being treated like a bone to be fought over by a pack of wolves.

But she wasn't an innocent victim. She had played her part. Spending money and never once wondering where it came from. She had betrayed Ethan, jumping at a better offer. There was no hiding from the truth. She knew Marty was spending far more than his business should have supplied, yet she'd never asked, 'Where is the money coming from, Marty?'

Over the past few days there had been plenty of opportunities to call for help. She could have phoned the police on numerous occasions, yet she had gone along with everything she'd been told to do. Not because of her love for Marty, but to protect her own hide. When things got ugly, she used alcohol as her way out. She'd been sleepwalking for so long that she barely remembered what it felt like to be fully awake.

"I'm awake now," she said to herself and was startled by a knock on the door.

"Beth?" Marty said. "Open the door."

She scrambled to her feet then tugged at her lower lip. Her mind jumped between questions. What did he want? What if she refused to let him in?

Refusing could lead to a scene. Marty might hammer on the door and Craig, hearing the commotion would rush out of the office. Marty might recognise Pike and then what? It just felt too risky. Too much could go wrong and she could get caught in the middle.

"Okay," she said and pulled the chair away.

Outwardly, he seemed calm and his usual self except for his jittering hands. The jitters had grown worse and were no longer ticks but more like little invisible tugs that were so slight, if someone didn't know him, they probably wouldn't have registered. But Beth knew him. She saw him and thought of invisible strings, jerking him like a resisting marionette. Seeing the jitters scared her.

"Why have you blocked the back door?" he asked.

She threw her hands up in exasperation. "Because I'm terrified. Because you said he's coming here," she said in the hope of drawing him out so he'd fill in the holes in her memory.

Marty surprised her by reaching out and pulling her into his arms. She let him hold her, unsure if it was the memory of better times or just human contact, but suddenly she felt emotional and wanted to weep.

"He won't come here. I told you. I've arranged for the meeting to be at cabin ten," he said.

A meeting? She wanted to laugh at the absurdity of it all. After committing a murder, Marty still saw himself as a businessman. If it wasn't so tragic, it would be funny. It was all so funny.

"You're safe in here as long as you stay put," he continued. "He won't come until it gets dark. I need you to watch the outside light on cabin ten. I'll leave it on. When I turn it off, it means it's over and you need to come back. If it doesn't turn off within fifteen minutes, I want you to hammer on the cabin door."

She thought of telling him that Pike was already there and posing as the maintenance man, but her gut told her to keep her suspicions to herself. For now, she needed to focus all her energy on Marty.

He pulled away and held her at arm's length so he could look into her eyes. "Have you got that?"

He was treating her like a child, eyeing her as if she was unstable or drunk. To be fair, she'd been both for the best part of three days but she forced herself to keep her frayed nerves under control.

"I've got it. Wait for the light to go off," she replied. "But if I'm going to be on my own in here, I need my phone."

He let go of her and shrugged. "Don't you have it?"

Inside she was screaming because she knew he had taken it, but when she spoke her voice sounded neutral. "It was charging in the bathroom. When I went to get it, it was gone."

"Well, I don't know where you left it," he replied and she was sure he was lying.

"We'll find it later. You don't need it now as long as you stick to the plan," he said.

He'd taken her phone; she was certain of it. He wanted her cut off from the world with no choice but to do as she was told. In some ways he had always wanted it that way. Now he no longer trusted her and that could be a problem – for her. She'd seen Lenton Hubbard's face and knew what her husband was capable of.

"You're right," she said and grimaced. "I was all over the place. I probably meant to charge it and put it down somewhere. It'll be flat by now." She had trouble stopping herself from babbling.

He smiled, but it was a patronising look. How had she never noticed how condescending he could be until now? Still, he seemed satisfied.

"We're okay, aren't we, pet? You're still with me?" His voice was soft, almost gentle, but she detected an underlying threat.

"Always," she answered with a grin that felt stretched to breaking point.

He kissed her – a long lingering kiss. She responded by going through the motions, clasping her hands around his neck while she tried not to think about Lenton Hubbard's pulverized head, his milky eyes filled with dirt and his body lying in a crudely dug grave.

A moment later Marty was gone, and she was left to wonder what, if anything, she really knew about the man she had shared a bed with for the past five years.

This time she did more than stare at the wine. She opened the bottle and poured a glass. She needed one to steady herself, not a large glass, only a few fingers. Taking care not to spill the wine, she pulled the chair back in front of the door and sat.

Who was Martin Jacobsen? A caring husband? A businessman? A drug dealer? A murderer? Who was the real Marty? Was he all of those things or had circumstances dictated his choices? Had he always been one thing hidden beneath another? That thought chilled her but no longer seemed farfetched.

She knew him, his likes, his dislikes, his favourite food, cologne, and TV shows. But knowing these things wasn't the same as understanding him or knowing his history.

Marty never talked about his family. He said it was because he'd been an only child and had never been close to his mother. According to him, his mother had died from emphysema. Until now it seemed to make sense. But did it? she wondered. Close or not, people couldn't help mentioning their childhood even if only in passing. Yet, she couldn't recall a single instance where Marty had revealed anything about his mother or his life while growing up.

All she knew was that he had always been good with numbers and that was the reason he had gone into finance. What did that tell her? Marty was secretive and she had been too self-involved to notice. She didn't even know what schools he had attended. How was that possible? If this was a film she was watching, she would be throwing up her hands and pointing out that only an idiot would marry someone they knew nothing about.

She took a sip of wine and shuddered at the taste. Did he grow up in Perth? Had he told her that or was it something she had assumed? Had she made the assumption out loud and he never corrected her? Why didn't she know? At their wedding, his only guests had been a handful of work friends. He didn't even have a best man.

Marty, something of an expert in historical trivia, had explained the best man's origin to her. The Germanic custom came about when women were in short supply and when a bachelor would seek out and capture a bride from a neighbouring community. Snatching up women was a two-man operation. So, the prospective groom would enlist the assistance of the best man available to help him stalk and capture an unsuspecting woman. A truly evolved man like Marty had detested the tradition. How could she not love him for having such noble beliefs?

The scar, she thought triumphantly. He did tell her something about his childhood. Marty told her about the scar after the first time they had made love. It was precious little, yet when he explained the burn, it seemed like he was opening up the deepest part of his soul. It became a painful truth that they shared. Now she wondered if the story was yet another lie.

On their first date when they had coffee, had the signs been there and she was just too young and short-sighted to see them? In hindsight, every moment of that first date and the ones that followed felt tainted. Falling in love, unable to help themselves, wracked with guilt over those they had hurt. Now, it all seemed so orchestrated.

She remembered that their first date had been set up without the exchange of phone numbers. Was that deliberate on his part? Without a phone number, he knew she wouldn't be able to text or call and back out. Another of his plans? A trap with her a willing victim? How had she ever been that young and foolish?

The past didn't matter anymore. Tonight was her focus. She had a feeling that Marty was telling the truth about one thing. After tonight, that would be it; one way or another.

Chapter Twenty-four

Lying on the bed and floating between infomercials and a restless doze, darkness crept in like a thief. By the time she noticed the change in the light, it was almost fully dark.

Before she got up and went over to the window, she heard a noise. Humming. Distant and like a mosquito. The hum ceased and there was silence cut only by the constant ghostly creaking of the swings. She couldn't see the playground, but knew it lay beyond the cabins. She wouldn't allow herself to picture the empty swings moving back and forth in the dark. Outside the window, there was nothing to see.

Was it her imagination or did she hear a bell tinkle? Could the breeze carry sound that far? It seemed possible in the dead of night. *Dead of night.* The words were ominous. She heard voices as well as faint and distant movement.

Five or ten minutes went by and then more noise. Something crashed and splintered. The noise was followed by an indistinct thud. Slightly unsteady on her feet, she leaned close to the window to gauge the origins of the noise. Her senses were dull, and she cursed herself for having a second glass of wine. When this was over, she might well have another problem to deal with, but that was a worry for another day.

Glancing to her right, she saw the outside light glowing under the eaves of cabin ten. To her left, she saw that the office lights were on. Her gaze wandered to the faint yellow beam that shone from a single solar light atop a pole near the end of the jetty. As soon as she glanced back at the office again, the lights went out.

Her stomach flipped. With only the half-moon shining on the lake and the dim glow from the jetty, the area between the office and the outside light of cabin ten lay in shadows. Among the shadows, a silhouette moved, and her mind went to the Moonlight Man.

Just as it had happened in the kitchen three days ago, her limbs went weak. Grabbing the window ledge, she was able to remain upright and track the shape.

She couldn't see the man clearly, but surmised that it was Craig, also known as Pike, making his way to cabin ten where Marty waited. Marty would give Pike the money plus a little extra and the debt would be paid.

Would it work? Would Pike be satisfied? She had no idea. She wanted to get to the office and use the phone and call for help. As she watched the shadows meld, she saw the silhouette on the move and with each of his strides, her heart roared like thunder. Leaning closer to the glass, her breath misted the surface.

She was letting this happen. It wouldn't end well, not for Marty or Pike. They would kill each other or if she was successful, the police would turn up and they would all be taken into custody. But she had run out of options and ideas.

Chapter Twenty-five

Beth had been on his mind more than he wanted to admit. This wasn't how it was supposed to go. If he'd learned anything from his time in prison, it was that the mind could be a dangerous thing. Letting your thoughts take you where they ought not go always led to trouble. Getting involved in other people's messes was trouble's welcome mat. He should have had that gem put on a T-shirt. Craig Williams: Trouble's Welcome Mat.

If he was smart, he would jump in his sister's car and drive home. He would do well to spend a few days in the surf and let the ocean wash her out of his head. But he'd never been that smart. A smart guy wouldn't lose his licence because he was blind drunk and speeding along the freeway while singing *Eye of the Tiger.* A really smart guy wouldn't get behind the wheel when he could barely see straight. A smart guy wouldn't drive without a licence, hit something and decide not to stop. He wouldn't have kept driving and singing along with the radio while telling himself it had been nothing but a wheelie bin on the side of the road. A man with a scrap of self-preservation wouldn't have ended up behind bars at thirty for reckless driving causing death.

Beth was dangerous; there was no doubt about it. A disaster, nervous, complicated, and probably a drunk. And *he* knew drunks. He'd been sober for thirteen years. Not a drop although he would have been lying if he said he hadn't come close on more than one occasion. One night, not long after his release and still on parole, he had what might be called a dark night of the soul. After wrestling with the idea of drinking himself to death, he bought a bottle. And why not? Death had to be better than facing the agony of slogging through the rest of his miserable life.

He watched that bottle for three gut-wrenching hours, mostly from the corner of his eye while pretending to watch television. Hours stealing glances at the thing and half-expecting it to somehow creep closer. Hours spent using the back of his hand to wipe sweat from his brow.

Fear stopped him from opening the cap and tipping the stuff out because he'd known that when the cap came off, the smell would be too much for him. Too much to resist. Whoever started the rumour that vodka had no smell was a black-hearted liar. One whiff and Craig would have been chugging like a baby latched onto a teat.

On his absurdly clichéd dark night of the soul, he experienced a stroke of genius. The sort of idea that only an addict would stumble upon while struggling during a bout of brain fever. Caught in this fever, he grabbed the bottle and ran out of the house so he could smash the thing against the side of the building. No licking it up if it was littered with broken glass and sinking into the sand.

The instant the bottle hit the bricks, the smell got him. Ethanol. A chemical scent mixed with berries, probably boysenberries. A piece of the glass must have bounced sideways because when he turned, almost blind with the need to escape, he stepped onto a large shard.

Crying out more from pure misery than the agony of pulling the bloody, slippery piece of glass out of his foot, he hobbled back inside, leaving a bloody trail across the cheap linoleum. The next morning when he woke, those red prints were waiting for him. A bloody path of shame.

Those footprints represented the destruction he was capable of once the smell got in his nose. They were a reminder of the old woman he'd killed while driving and swigging vodka. He was sober now, but he would always be a drunk at heart.

Two drunks – even former drunks – equalled disaster. Beth was also married. Not a great marriage he suspected, but that turmoil only made what he was thinking worse. He was thinking about wading into her personal chaos.

He should be running like his ass was on fire, but damn it, she was in over her head. Any fool could see that. She had that cornered look in her dark eyes – eyes that reminded him of rich, dusky coffee and of early morning air and the sandy shore he had come to love.

The husband was the problem. Craig didn't believe the story about the bruises on her face. The idea of the bloke in the fancy Mazda putting his hands on Beth made Craig want to throttle him. It was an urge he couldn't allow himself to give in to. Still, something wasn't right between them and it didn't seem like an average marital tiff. Not even a knock-down, dragged-out, dish-smashing barney, for that matter. It was in her eyes – danger. Craig could practically smell it and its smell was almost as intoxicating as vodka.

As he was about to lock the office door for the night, he thought the best thing was for him to leave Beth alone. All he could add to her situation was grief. Hadn't there been enough grief at White Mist Lake? The sound of an engine cut off his thoughts. A car was approaching.

Odd because there were no bookings and if there were, 7:00 p.m. was well past check-in time. The only people who had a reason to be on the private road that led to the retreat were guests, or maybe some lost stumblebum looking for a way out of the forest. Or it could be Tracy, he realised. A friend might be dropping her home.

He left the door unlocked and waited as he watched the parking lot. A second later, the engine cut off and the night returned to silence. If whoever was driving the car had been heading away from the retreat, the hum would have gradually diminished. But no, the engine had definitely stopped which meant someone had pulled up just beyond the office.

As the minutes ticked by, he wondered if he'd been mistaken about the engine. Could the car have driven off without him hearing? His questions were answered when a figure, large and clearly male, appeared just outside of the light that spilled from the office windows and door. Whoever the man was, he was going to great lengths to approach without being heard. The man, dressed in dark clothing, moved with the deliberate caution of someone who didn't want to be seen or heard. Bad news, however Craig looked at it. But if the intruder was intent on stealing or vandalising, Craig owed it to his sister to act. Tracy had enough to cope with without coming back to discover that the retreat had been trashed.

Fearing this wasn't going to end well, Craig went against his better instincts, which usually erred on the side of 'mind your own damn business', and opened the office door.

"You looking for something?" he asked, pitching his voice so the man would know he'd been spotted.

If he was up to no good, and that clearly seemed the case, being seen might be enough to send him running. Problem solved.

The sound of Craig's voice didn't send the intruder running, but it did make the figure freeze. A full three seconds ticked by while neither of them moved. In that time, Craig considered going back inside and calling the cops. But ex-cons who called the police somehow ended up being the ones taken into custody. While he was no stranger to a cell, the thought of entering one again made his chest tighten until breathing felt more like drowning.

The stranger's head turned, a small tilting movement that should have been impossible for Craig to see in the dark, but see it he did. A chill coming off the lake touched Craig's skin and suddenly calling the cops seemed like a pretty good idea.

"My car broke down." The man's voice was deep and coarse at the same time. The voice rekindled memories Craig wished he could forget – memories of cells and other similar men.

"Can I use your phone? Mine's flat."

Craig's thoughts jumped from the cops to his father's shotgun that was stashed away at the back of his sister's wardrobe. He was sure he remembered seeing a box of shells back there too. It seemed funny that the old man had a shotgun yet had used a hammer on Craig's mother before hanging himself. The old memories nagged at Craig's thoughts, kicked off by the way the man's head had moved in the dark. The last time Craig saw his father, he'd had that same peculiar tilt to his head – a tilt that suggested he could hear something on the wind.

"No problem," Craig said. "Stay out here and I'll go and grab it."

The stranger moved into the light and walked to the steps that led to the office. Craig tensed, half-expecting the man to come at him. The stranger stopped at the foot of the steps and smiled. It was a strange, humourless dragging up of the lips. A smile that said, *I know I'm scaring you and I'm enjoying it.*

Craig stood his ground above the stranger, looking down and taking in the man's size: tall and wide across the shoulders. Craig also noted that size-wise he was more than a match for the other man. He studied the man's self-assured stance and saw eyes that were hungry for violence – eyes that were scanning Craig for weakness. He knew this type all too well. In prison he spent years keeping his head down, avoiding men like this stranger.

"You're a lifesaver," the stranger said, sounding more mocking than grateful.

Craig held the man's gaze for a second then turned and went inside. He had no intention of letting the stranger use his phone and every intention of grabbing the shotgun and showing the guy the business end while telling him to get the hell off the property. Once the asshole got moving, Craig would think about calling the cops although there wouldn't be much to report, just some lowlife trying his luck.

Leaving the man outside, Craig crossed the office and entered the back room. He paused long enough to grab his phone and shove it in his pocket. Before he had time to reach Tracy's bedroom, he heard a sound that made his gut clench with dread: the shop bell.

There was no time to hesitate. He had to act and go for the gun or find another weapon. His eyes darted around the sitting room and landed on a thick glass jar that housed a scented candle.

"Did you find it?" the stranger asked from the entrance to the back room.

Craig, holding the candle at his side and slightly behind his right leg, turned.

"The phone? That's what you're looking for, right?" the stranger asked.

"I told you to wait outside," Craig said, not bothering to keep anger out of his voice. And he did feel anger. That and fear.

"Yeah, well, it's cold out there." The stranger dropped the pretence of pleasantries and now sounded belligerent.

"If you need the phone so desperately," Craig began, "you can use the one out there in the office, but make it quick. I'm closing up."

The man didn't answer right away. Craig sensed that the situation was about to escalate.

"No problem," the man said then turned back to the office.

Craig continued to weigh the gravity of the situation and the need for the shotgun. Although some of the tension had left Craig's muscles when the man had turned to leave. The guy was creepy, but maybe he really *did* just want to use the phone. He'll probably hit me up for ten bucks on his way out, Craig thought wryly. Still pondering his next move, he heard a clang followed by the clatter of objects hitting the floor.

Without hesitating, Craig rushed into the office. "What the hell are—"

Before he could finish the question, he saw that the man was holding the old rotary phone. The cord had been cut and dangled at his side. Craig stepped back, but it was too late. The phone was already closing in on him. The heavy antique smashed into the side of Craig's head and the world stuttered in and out of blackness.

Staggering as the stranger continued to approach, Craig touched his scalp, wide-eyed at the sight of blood on his fingers. The stranger's face was stark with brutal pleasure as he loomed over Craig and lifted the phone a second time. I'm about to die in the spot my mother was bludgeoned to death, Craig thought.

Desperate to defend himself and stop the attack, Craig backhanded the jar and clipped the stranger's jaw. Blood dripped from Craig's brows and clouded his vision, but he saw the phone drop and the man grab his face.

With the strength draining from Craig's limbs, when he moved it was with a swaying gait. While his body buckled, his mind was firmly fixed on the shotgun.

Without knowing how badly he had injured the stranger or how long before another blow landed, Craig ran for the bedroom on legs that weren't cooperating. Blood not only filled his eyes, but pounded in his ears.

"You should have stayed in your office," the stranger said in a slushy voice.

Craig didn't look back, but hoped he had messed the man's mouth up. He hoped it hurt like hell. But the shotgun was more important. If he could reach it, there was a chance he would be able to put a stop to the attack.

He made it to the bedroom. Behind him, the man thumped across the floor to catch him. When Craig's hand reached the doorframe and there was only a few more metres to go, a blow landed on his back. The impact knocked the breath out of his lungs and Craig collapsed.

The stranger stood over him then dragged him onto his back and snatched at his pockets. Craig tried to bat the man off with his one working arm, but his attempts to fight were sluggish and pathetic.

The man took Craig's phone then stepped over him. In a desperate attempt to stop the guy, Craig grabbed at his leg. The stranger turned back and before moving out of Craig's field of vision, kicked him in the hip. The final assault sent a shaft of agony through Craig's side.

While fighting for breath and still thinking of the gun, Craig tried to get up, but nausea and dizziness crashed over him and he fell back. As he struggled to breathe, the lights went out and darkness surrounded him. Seconds later the shop bell tinkled.

Chapter Twenty-six

The dark figure neared cabin ten. His silhouette froze, making it impossible to tell where he ended and the shadows began. Time to move, Beth told herself, but her fingers were reluctant to release the windowsill. She was afraid, not just for herself, but for Marty. Why did she still feel that wrench? That agonising pull of emotion? After everything he'd done, Marty continued to exert power over her.

The answer came to her with almost perfect clarity. It was never the lifestyle or the money; it was the darkness that drew her in. Danger, uncertainty, excitement; she craved it. She hesitated, determined to resist it, yet oddly it was that self-destructive pull that got her moving. If she didn't go now, she would be lost.

She headed out the back door and moved around the cabin, hugging the walls. Like a shock of cold water, the night air had a sobering effect. Up ahead, the light on the jetty loomed out of the mist and she used it as her anchor and darted left.

Even in the moonlight the office was discernible. She crossed the distance with care not wanting to repeat the fall she'd taken earlier. It was only when she reached the office door that it occurred to her it might be locked. Pressing her lips together, she tried the handle and the door swung in.

She hissed out a curse as the shop bell jangled in the dark. Cabin ten sat too far away. It was doubtful anyone would have heard the clang. Still, she turned and peered through the glass door to make sure no one was approaching. No knife-wielding madman running towards the office was a good sign. Not that she could see much through the shadows and trees, not to mention the ghostly mist coming off the lake.

Turning back to the counter, she realised she wouldn't get far without light and instinctively reached for her pocket before remembering that Marty had her phone. With no other option, she shuffled forward. Half a metre in, her shoes crunched on broken glass and a cold chill skipped across her shoulders. Something was off.

The phone should be straight ahead. She couldn't remember if the old rotary dial phone had a cord, but prayed it was still functioning. Something splintered under her shoe. Had Pike smashed the place up before he left as a final fuck you to add to whatever else he'd done to the missing woman?

Feeling her way around the counter, she fumbled for the phone and came up empty. She was about to try the walls in search of a light switch when she heard movement inside the living quarters.

Her hand halted its search and hung frozen in the darkness. While holding her breath, she listened and heard a groan. Someone was in the back room.

Her first impulse was to run. She was turning when her mind caught up to her panicked reflexes. Pike couldn't be in two places at once. She thought back to the racket she heard minutes ago. Something had crashed. Could it have been a struggle or some kind of attack?

She squeezed her eyes shut and took a second to gather the courage to investigate. What if she'd been wrong about

Craig and he was hurt? The part of her that cared only about her own fears screamed for her to flee. The urge was powered by adrenaline that made her hands tremble.

Another noise, this one a pained-sounding grunt. She stepped closer to the curtain then used a hand to search for a light switch. Momentarily blinded by the sudden glare, the first thing she saw was the rotary phone lying on the floor. Blinking, she realised the antique was smeared with blood – fresh blood.

Craig lay on the other side of the room with his legs splayed as he struggled to sit up.

Beth covered her mouth to hold back a shriek then hurried to his side. Blood coated half his face. There was a laceration on the left side of his head where his scalp had been split open. She'd been so wrong about him. Craig was never the enemy, just a kind man that had tried to help her.

"What happened?" she asked automatically. A stupid question because she knew exactly what had happened. The real Pike had done this.

What she saw in Craig's eyes stabbed at her heart. He looked terrified, hurt, and in shock. She had brought this on him. This was his reward for getting involved in her mess, for trying to help her.

"A man," Craig said. "When I heard… I thought you were him coming back."

He tried to sit up, but could only get on one elbow before coughing and sliding back until he lay prone on the floor.

"He took my phone," Craig continued.

As the weight of his words sank in, she noticed more blood trickling from the corner of his mouth. "Are you hurt anywhere else?" she asked, too worried to touch him for fear she might make things worse.

Craig's eyelids fluttered.

"Craig, stay awake," she snapped and grabbed his shoulder.

He winced. "My back."

Beth reached under him and felt warmth on her fingers and realised he was bleeding from his back.

"I'm going to look at your back," she said. "Can you lift up?"

Craig moved his head and she took the action for a nod.

"Count of three," she said hoping she could cope with whatever it was she was about to see.

On three he shifted as she pushed. Craig panted out a sharp breath and Beth got a glimpse of his sodden shirt and the pool of blood he'd been lying in. He'd been stabbed and needed help fast.

"Stay here," she said. "I'll be back."

She got up and rushed across the room then came back with a rug and draped it over him, tucking it under his chin. Craig was frighteningly pale and quiet.

Next, she hurried to the office only to find the computer smashed and its screen lying on the floor on the far side of the counter. No chance of using the internet to call for help. Light spilling out of the back room gave enough illumination for her to make her way to the front door. She threw the bolt and locked them in. If Pike came back, it wouldn't hold for long, but it was something. She grabbed the rotary phone hoping to find an outlet to plug it into only for her to see that the receiver had been ripped from the base.

"Damn, damn," she muttered. Pike had thought of everything.

The adrenaline that had been pushing her forward was still rolling, but it was also making it difficult to settle and focus. All she knew was that it was no longer about putting an end to the three-day nightmare she'd been living. It was now about Craig and getting him help. They were cut off, isolated from the world, but there had to be another way. There was always another way.

She went to the door and cupped her hands to the glass. The outside light still burned over cabin ten. The meeting between Pike and Marty was still in progress or Marty was unable to give the signal. If it was the latter, she couldn't be sure what she felt. Grief? Sorrow? Relief? Right now, she was numb to all those things.

When she returned to the back room, she drew the curtain hoping if Pike passed the office, he wouldn't see the light. Craig's eyes were closed. What she could see of his face looked waxy and bleached of colour. He was losing too much blood.

She bypassed him and went to the kitchen, noticing that like the cabins, the living quarters had a back door. It gave her an idea. Pulling open drawers, some with so much force that they clattered to the floor and spilled cutlery across the room, she found a stack of tea towels. She ran one under the cold tap and then folded the other into a pad. Then rummaging through cupboards, she found a first aid kit on the top shelf of the pantry.

"Craig?" She snapped her fingers in front of his face and his eyes opened. "Don't close your eyes," she said as she folded the damp tea towel and placed it on his scalp.

With no time to waste, she opened the first aid kit and grabbed a few bandages. Using her teeth, she tore packets open.

"I need to bandage your head," she said. As gently as possible, she wrapped the gauze around his head wound.

Next, she assisted him into a half-sitting position and tried not to gag when she got a clear look at the gash on his back. Pressing the tea towel pad against the wound, she did her best to fix the dressing in place. It was a sloppy job, but she hoped it would at least stem the bleeding.

Throughout the process, Craig hadn't uttered a word and she was worried he was about to lose consciousness.

"There's a shotgun in the wardrobe," he said as she helped him lie down again. "Shells too." As he spoke, more blood ran out of his mouth and painted his lips red.

A shotgun. The idea of touching such a weapon was repulsive, but she knew firsthand what Pike was capable of and she only had to look at Craig to realise they needed protection. She'd helped bury a body, now wasn't the time for her crazy scruples.

It took only a few minutes of shoving clothes and shoes aside to find the shotgun. It was bigger and heavier than she expected and felt cold, like dead weight in her hands. Maybe that was a good thing. If it came to it, just pointing the thing at Pike might be enough to scare him off.

Craig gave her a halting lesson on how to load the shotgun and release the safety. At times it seemed as though he was drifting away from her and fading in and out. She loaded the weapon and placed it on the sofa with the barrel pointing away from them. It was silly, but she felt that the gun was another sinister player in this endless ordeal – a being with a life of its own. She didn't trust the thing not to go off on its own accord.

"Craig?" His eyes were closed and his lids had taken on a lilac hue. "Craig," she tried again and this time he blinked and opened his eyes. "We'll go out the back door and take your car. Once we get to the shop, I'll break a window. If we're in luck, I'll find a phone and set off an alarm at the same time."

If he was following the plan, he gave no indication. Beth thought of Lenton and promised herself that she wouldn't let Craig end up as another casualty of Marty's business dealings.

"I'll help you stand," she said and tried to slide her hand under his shoulder.

Craig groaned and shook his head. "Can't. You go. Take the shotgun. Keys on coffee table."

She'd been so frantic, rushing around and coming up with a plan, but now the will to keep pushing fizzled out like a melted birthday candle.

He was telling her to leave him when they both knew he might not survive the time it would take her to go for help. Sagging, she sat back on her heels and her bloody hands fell limp in her lap. She couldn't hold back the sobs.

She had been wandering through not only the last few days, but years of her life. All the time she thought Marty was the weak one, but it was her all along. Weak, helpless, complicit, unable to think for herself, and now when the stakes were high, she had crumbled and didn't have the strength to fight.

"Go," Craig said. His weary eyes implored her.

Beth pressed the heels of her hands into her eyes, trying to bring her emotions under control. Craig was suffering, yet she was the one breaking down.

Sucking in air, she reined her emotions in. Deep breaths helped as she lifted the edge of her jumper and used the part that wasn't stained with blood to scrub the tears away. Craig couldn't walk and there was no way she could get him on his feet, let alone shoulder his weight. No use wailing like a child. Time to suck it up, buttercup, she told herself.

Before leaving, she tucked the blanket back under his chin and resisted the urge to plant a kiss on his cheek.

"Try to stay awake," she told him. "I'm going to turn the overhead light off, but put the lamp on."

So he won't know you're alive and come back, she thought, but didn't say.

Craig wasn't looking at her, but his eyes were open. As he breathed, his lungs made gurgling sounds. Sounds that she wouldn't let herself dwell on.

"I'll be as quick as I can," she said, wanting to say more, but time was ticking and what else was there to say? Any promises would have sounded hollow. Instead, she adjusted the lights, picked up the shotgun, grabbed the keys, then left through the back door.

Chapter Twenty-seven

Grateful for the moonlight, she edged her way around the back of the building. The little red car stood out in the dark and she scurried to the driver's door then crouched with the barrel of the shotgun pointing down. She planned on driving slowly at first and with the headlights off until she reached the private road. Navigating in the dark meant running the risk of ending up in the lake. She wavered at that thought, but it was a chance she would have to take.

With her hand on the car door, she peered toward cabin ten and saw that the outside light had been turned off. Marty had given the signal. Did that mean that Pike was gone? Had he taken the money and slithered back into the night?

She dropped low so she was half-hidden by the car. Her eyes adjusted to the darkness and so far, she saw no signs of movement around the lake.

Her phone was in the cabin. If Pike was gone, she could demand Marty return the mobile so she could call for an ambulance. It was a risky move. Marty had become increasingly unstable. Who knew how he'd react to the news that Pike had attacked Craig? But if she tried for her phone instead of driving to the shops, Craig would have a better chance. Even if she made it to the shop there was no guarantee that she'd find a phone. Out here in the back of beyond, some shop owners might not see the need for an alarm or a landline phone.

If there was no way to alert the authorities at one of the shops, she would have to drive to Bunbury. Even at speed it would be a thirty-minute drive and another thirty for help to arrive. Would Craig survive that long? She was driving herself mad with possibilities and talking herself in and out of every decision while Craig was likely to bleed to death.

"Come on," she whispered, trying to coax herself into a choice.

Getting to her phone was the best option. Marty would need careful handling, but she had become an expert in tiptoeing around him. With the decision made, she headed toward cabin ten. She took the shotgun, deciding it was too dangerous to leave it lying around. Besides, who knew where Pike was lurking or if he had truly left the retreat? She hoped to God that Marty wouldn't do anything that would push her into using the weapon.

She stepped carefully, weaving her way closer to empty cabins. Maybe she was being overly cautious, but after the things she'd seen caution seemed prudent.

Light filtered out of the cabin window in a warm glow that turned the hut into an island amid a sea of darkness. Beth took slow steps, treading each board with care. By the time she reached the door, her heart was racing and despite the cold, her fingers felt slippery on the gun.

She was about to open it when she heard voices. Raised voices. Marty was talking. Beth stepped to the window and peered in through a chink in the curtains. What she saw obliterated everything she thought she knew about Marty and left her trembling with shock.

Pike – it had to be him – had a rope around his neck that had been tied to the foot of the bed. Marty stood over

Pike, brandishing a knife. The cold and fear slowed Beth's thoughts and made it difficult to make sense of the scene.

Yet, as she watched Marty rolling his shoulders and dancing on the balls of his feet, it became clear that he was pumping himself up like an athlete preparing for a difficult challenge. Was this how he had readied himself to murder Lenton Hubbard? One thing was clear. She barely recognised her own husband.

"Don't." She threw open the door without thought or planning.

Both men looked surprised by her sudden appearance.

"Beth." Marty's eyes flicked from her face to the shotgun. "I got him." He looked relieved to see her, proudly displaying Pike like a prized trophy. "I knew you'd come," he said. "I wanted to give him the money, but he tried to attack me."

He stopped speaking and took in the blood on her jumper and the shotgun again. For a moment he appeared confused and hesitant. She waited for him to question her, but his restless eyes were already jumping away from her. He seemed beyond comprehending anything other than his own thoughts.

"We don't have a choice," he continued about Pike. "He'll never see reason. We'll never be safe. You get that, don't you?"

Beth shook her head, grappling to keep up with what Marty was proposing.

"No," she whispered. "No," she said louder. "No more, Marty."

"He's lying!" Pike raged in a hoarse and strangled voice as the rope dug into his neck. There was blood on his face, but she recognised the timbre of his words from the night he'd broken into their house.

"He was waiting with the rope and jumped me," Pike said. "He's nuts." As he spoke, his jaw worked at an odd angle.

"Shut up," Marty growled, pointing the knife at Pike. When Marty spoke to Beth again, he softened his tone. "We can go home once it's done. Go on with our lives. If I don't finish this now, he'll come after us."

"Did he tell you what he did?" Pike asked, somehow managing to sound calm and still in control.

Looking into Pike's emotionless eyes made Beth's skin crawl. It was days since he'd assaulted her, but she could still feel the blade on her skin. It was like an invisible scar that burned cold instead of hot. She thought of Craig and what Pike did to him, and a dark place in her heart wanted Marty to kill him. Her body was a solid lump of hatred that demanded satisfaction.

"It wasn't about the money. That was part of it, but the money was just business," Pike continued. "We would have only come after *him* for the money." Pike couldn't move his head, but his eyes travelled in Marty's direction then back to Beth's. "*He* made it personal."

Marty lunged forward and plunged the knife in Pike's thigh. Beth's scream matched Pike's cry of agony as Marty twisted the blade and blood covered his hand.

"Stop it!" Beth lifted the gun with trembling hands and pleaded. "Please, Marty, stop."

"Now look what you made me do," Marty said and yanked at the knife. It made a fleshy slurping sound as it left Pike's leg.

Beth gagged and her vision became watery and blurred.

"Did he tell you he gave Len's nineteen-year-old niece heroin? He couldn't keep his hands off her. From the minute he saw her, he was sniffing around like a fucking dog." Pike gasped and pressed his hand to the knife wound. "She's in a coma." The words came out in an agonised rush. "How do you think we got in your house?" He grinned. "He gave her a key. He had her there when you were out. He had her in your bed," Pike said with a strained laugh.

"No. That's a lie," Marty said then turned to Beth with the bloody knife gripped in his hand. "I love you, Beth. The girl, Carrie, she was a druggie. She meant nothing to me. You're my whole world." His eyes were wild and feverish. The knife dripped blood onto the rug. "After this we can try for a baby. We'll be a proper family just like you've always wanted."

They were the words she had waited so long to hear, but now they made her feel sick. The idea of having a baby with him turned her stomach. She had no reason to believe Pike yet she did.

"I want my phone," Beth said and aimed the shotgun at Marty. "I mean it." Her hands shook so badly she could barely keep the weapon steady. "I have to call my mum." The last part came out with a sob.

"First we have to sort this out and then we'll do whatever you want," Marty said, nodding.

"He picked her up at a party," Pike continued. "Len's a yobbo, but Carrie was a good kid. She wanted to be one of those dental nurses. Now she'll be lucky if she can ever feed herself again."

Pike's words snatched Beth's breath away. Heat settled on her like a scald. Connections were clicking into place and another layer of the Marty she thought she knew slipped away.

"I can't do this," Beth said. Hysteria had crept into her voice.

Without warning, Marty grabbed the barrel of the shotgun and wrenched it out of her hands. He spun it then raised the barrel as Beth screamed and darted for the door.

Chapter Twenty-eight

There was nowhere to go and nothing but night and endless isolation. She ran for the shadows as her breath blew back cold on her face. Unsure if Marty was behind her, she headed for the blur of bushes and trees that ringed part of the lake.

By the time she reached the shrubs, she was winded from the burst of speed and had to stop and put her hands on her knees. There were no sounds of pursuit. Her dark jeans and blue jumper blended into the darkness. With enough cover around her to keep her from being seen, she turned and watched the cabin.

She was supposed to bring Craig help, but like with everything else, she had failed. The outside light turned on in front of cabin ten. Whatever had delayed Marty, he was coming now.

Frenzied, she stumbled into the bushes. Branches clawed at her face and clothes as she pushed forward. Thorns tore at her cheek and burned a trail across her skin, but she kept going until she broke free and found herself on sandy ground and at the patch of the bank where she had discovered the scrap of cherry-red fabric.

"Beth?" Marty's voice sounded overly loud in the deserted retreat. "Why are you running? I wasn't going to hurt you. We're in this together." He sounded close.

He was lying. Everything was a lie. Their marriage, his job, and what happened to Lenton. The things Pike said about the girl named Carrie resonated, but were they more lies? There was no earthly reason for her to believe Pike, but she did. Not because he was any more credible than Marty, but because of the things Marty said when he talked in his sleep.

Carrie, not carry. In a fevered dream, Marty had called out the girl's name. Beth had naively assumed he'd been talking about carrying something when in truth he'd probably been trying to lift a metaphorical weight. The reality was simple. What he'd done to Carrie haunted him and gave him a reason to dream about Lenton Hubbard's teenage niece. Or maybe he was calling for the girl because he longed for her. Beth no longer believed Marty was capable of love, but she knew that once he set his sights on something, he became obsessed.

She crouched and thought of the way he lifted the barrel of the shotgun. The way his hazel eyes took on an emotionless and predatory quality as he had snatched the weapon out of her hands.

"Come on, pet. You'll hurt yourself running around in the dark." His voice sounded reasonable and concerned. "Come inside and talk to me. Pike was lying to you – trying to get in your head. Don't let him come between us."

A chill rippled off the lake and through her clothes. He was close and searching. His shoes whispered over the dewy grass. A light played over the bushes. Marty was hunting her, scouring the trees. If she stayed put, he'd find her, but she was hemmed in by the water.

"Beth, stop this," he called from somewhere off to her left. "There's no need to hide. This is ridiculous." Concern had been replaced with impatience.

With no other choice, she kept low and scurried toward the water. As the cold shock crept over her shoes and up her legs, she held her breath to keep from making a sound.

To her right, she saw the light over the jetty and kept moving. With her arms out in front of her, she was careful to minimise the disturbance on the surface of the lake. She waded further and was surprised by how quickly the water deepened. In seconds she was shoulder deep. Pulling in a breath, she submerged herself in the dark water.

The world above vanished as she swam blindly and groped her way through the murky depths. If she was headed in the right direction, the jetty should be close.

Progress was painfully slow. Her water-logged clothes and shoes dragged her down until she struggled not only to swim, but to keep from sinking deeper. With each stroke, her fingers tangled through slimy reeds and over moss-covered debris. Thoughts of meat hungry, snake-necked turtles with sharp claws made her eyes dart in all directions. With almost zero visibility, anything could have been approaching her. Finally, with her lungs constricting and burning with the need for air, her hand hit something solid, and she risked breaking the surface.

Slowly and with her eyes and nose first, she emerged. She was at the far edge of the jetty. A sweet, rotten stench came off the water. It filled her mouth and made her throat contract. Her head bobbed as the area around the small wharf came into view.

"Beth?" Marty's voice, flat and insistent echoed off the lake.

She caught sight of his torchlight and quickly ducked, letting the water swallow her. Beneath the surface, she used the old wooden pylons to pull herself under the jetty before coming up for air.

Peering up, she saw bars of light filtering through the gaps in the boards. Something brushed her legs, but she kept her attention focused on the jetty above. A moment passed and then another. Perhaps he'd given up or had moved on to search another area.

She allowed herself to hope. If she could get to Craig's car without being seen, she'd do what she should have when she had the chance and get the hell out of this godforsaken place. She was considering swimming for the banks when the wood above thumped with the sound of heavy footfalls. Her teeth chattered from the cold, but she went under a third time.

Eyes open and with faint light filtering into the water, she caught movement from the corner of her eye. A water snake weaved toward her. Her heart dropped a beat before she realised that what she actually saw was a rope that had been laced around the pylon. One of the lengths caught and tangled around her arm. As she struggled to pull free, a mass appeared out of the depths.

The bobbing shape lunged toward her and Beth saw eyes that were empty and black. A face bloated and grey emerged in the green-black water. It pressed closer until the monstrous creature was nose to nose with her. A turtle clung to the dead, doughy face like a giant parasite.

Terror overtook every other instinct and Beth pushed backwards, sinking deeper as a silent scream bubbled out of her mouth. The more she struggled, the tighter the rope clasped her arm. She sank, struggling until her feet hit the soft bed of the lake and she was able to push up with all the strength she could muster.

When she broke the surface, she gasped for air and her head struck the underside of the jetty. Dazed, she sank again. There was silence and her body became weightless.

She was on the river with her face turned up to the sky while her limbs floated on the gentle toss of the current. There was a taste on her tongue, not the sweet flavour of oranges, but of rank brackish water.

Her eyes snapped opened and she pushed against the water. Her limbs felt grotesquely sluggish. There was no up or down, just the spasming of her lungs. Panic made her struggle harder. Above, she caught a glimpse of the half-moon – a wisp of light that called to her through the depths. Suddenly, the way was clear. She flipped her feet like a duck and ascended.

She was out and as she gulped at air, she realised she had cleared the jetty and was in the open. There was a second of relief before she floundered, realising she was exposed.

With no time to move, hands grabbed her shoulders and dragged her backward then up. Her body scraped over wood and then she was dumped on her back. The half-moon viewed her like a mocking eye.

"You shouldn't have done that," Marty said, leaning over her.

"There's a body," she stammered. "A body under the water."

He was crouched beside her. Under the sickly yellow light of the jetty, his face looked like a ghoulish mask of angles that transformed him into something alien.

"Why did you have to go under there?" he asked with what sounded like sorrow.

Beth sat up confused by his response. "Did you hear what I said? I think it's the woman that checked us in. Tracy. She's under the jetty."

She looked into his face and could hardly believe her own thoughts. Up until that moment, all of Marty's actions made an insane kind of sense. His choices were those of a desperate man, but the retreat owner? A woman that had done nothing more than hand him the keys to their cabin? Why hurt someone who had nothing to do with their predicament?

"You killed her?" she asked in a disbelieving voice.

Marty smiled then made a tutting sound. She stared at him with dumb horror as the cold finally reached her bones. The expression on his face was familiar: the unnatural calm before the storm. She wanted to run, but her sodden clothes weighed her down and he was close enough to simply grab her.

"Why?" Beth asked, shivering.

"It wasn't like that," he said. "She turned up at the cabin on that first evening. You were taking a nap." He moved onto his haunches. After getting comfortable, he picked up his torch and let it dangle in his hand.

Suddenly, he was the old Marty settling in and about to share a great story. He'd always been a storyteller, she realised, and she his adoring audience. She gave him what he wanted and curled her legs to the side. Shifting into the position made it easier to get up and run, while trying to make the movement appear casual.

"She had more maps for me. God that woman liked to talk. Going on and on about places of interest, treating me like some sort of drop-kick tourist." He shook his head. "She just wouldn't get the message. Finally, I thought I'd given her the brush off, but then she spotted the ants on the car. Little fuckers."

He thumped his thigh so violently that Beth winced.

"If she'd just shut her mouth and kept walking. But she started carrying on about infestations, saying she'd call her brother and have him take a look at our cabin. Before I could stop her, she had her hands on the boot." He paused. "I just pushed her. I didn't even know I was going to do it until my hands were on her back. She fell and hit her head on the bottom step." He tossed the torch into his other hand then dragged his right hand over his neck. "I knew it was bad because of the noise her head made when it hit. But what could I do?"

What could he do? She replayed the words in her mind. Call an ambulance. Try to help her. Anything besides throwing her in the lake. It all started coming together. Marty must have written the note and cancelled the other bookings. In doing that he had killed two birds with one stone. Craig wouldn't worry about Tracy being absent from the retreat and there would be no other guests to get in the way. He seemed to be waiting for her reaction. They were like two strangers now, each unsure of the other's intentions.

"This isn't you, Marty," she said, hoping he would blame the tremor in her voice on the cold water. "I know you didn't mean for things to go this far."

He nodded in agreement then tossed the torch back and forth. If only his face would come out of the shadows so she could see his eyes.

"It was an accident," he repeated. "I told you."

"I know. I know," she said. "I get it. Really, I do. You didn't mean to hurt anyone." She shifted her position again. "No one would blame you, but—"

"But you ran away from me," he finished for her.

"I wasn't running from you," she said. "It was seeing Pike. I got scared, that's all."

Marty let out a long breath. "I wish I could believe you, pet. I really do."

"Marty—"

"You ran, Beth. You were running away when you were in that maintenance guy's car yesterday. Do you think I'm stupid?" He leaned closer and his face came into the light. With a sly calculating look in his eyes there was little trace of the man she knew. This time the shiver that wracked her body had nothing to do with the cold. "No use lying, pet."

Beth didn't want to waste energy crying, but the tears kept coming. Time was running out. She heard it in the fatalistic tone of his voice. No more jitters for Marty. He had made a decision. He was going to hurt her. She could almost feel the violence coming off him and rolling toward her like the mist coming off the lake.

"I ran because you wouldn't come with me. This place." She waved a hand at the lake. "It's bad for us. Things have gone wrong from the moment we arrived. What happened with Tracy proves it. It's not you. It's this place."

A change came over his expression. He was listening, looking hopeful. That's good, she thought. He was reconsidering his next move. What she needed was time and a little distance. She needed the blood to circulate through her numb limbs so she could run.

"If we leave and just go away, things will be better," she continued. "I keep thinking about that day at the river." She forced a smile and Marty smiled back. It was an unattractive smile that almost put her off track, but she managed to keep going. "Before the wedding, do you remember?"

He blinked and she saw tears in his eyes. If she could keep him talking and find a reason to stand, she'd have a head start.

"We were eating oranges and you said, 'You're my home now.'" She could feel the car keys bunched in her pocket. "Marty, you're *my* home too. I want us to be like that again."

He wiped his eyes with the back of his hand. As he moved, she rolled to her side then stood. He started to rise, but she held up a hand and signalled for him to stop.

"I want us to have a fresh start. Leave everything behind. The house. The business." She turned in a half-circle with her arms out. It was a dramatic gesture, but it gave her another couple of metres. "That's the only way it'll work," she continued and took another step away from him. "I'll ask my mother to take Angel and then it will be just the two of us again, like it was in the beginning."

Still holding the torch, he let his head fall into his hands and his shoulders shuddered. He was breaking down and sobbing. This might be her only chance.

"You had me for a second," he said then lifted his head and she saw he wasn't crying, but laughing. "You went too far with that bit about Angel." He pointed the end of the torch at her. "I'm not an idiot. I know you'd never leave that mutt behind."

Chapter Twenty-nine

Beth's heart rocketed into her throat. Not giving him time to get to his feet, she spun around and ran. The ground was dark and without the office light everything was a blur. Moving with as much speed as she could summon, she sprinted toward the office. Behind her, Marty's feet pounded the ground with the thundering weight of a galloping boar.

Her right foot came down on a stone and her ankle wobbled, but held. She reached into her pocket and fumbled out the keys. If she could unlock the car doors, there was a chance she could jump inside and engage the lock. She'd drive and, if she had to, mow Marty down.

With the keys clutched in her fist, she pressed blindly at the buttons. Ahead, the Hyundai's lights flashed and she realised she had run off course and needed to veer left. He was so close. She could feel his weight crashing through the air and hear his grunting breaths. She imagined his hand reaching out to grab her.

Beth turned suddenly, hoping the movement would throw Marty off stride so she could gain a second. The car was less than ten metres away when something thumped into her shoulder and her left arm sagged. She cried out as

Marty snatched her jumper and swung her sideways. Turning and falling, she hit the ground.

Within seconds he was over her with his arm raised, lashing her with savage blows across the back. Between strikes, she rolled to the side and the torch landed on her ribs. Something cracked and a shaft of agony sliced through her chest.

Her breathing became impaired. Still, she cried out. "Marty, please don't." But it was no good. He wasn't listening to her.

She scampered back trying to avoid the onslaught when he struck her again.

"I gave you everything, Beth," he said through clenched teeth. "And you threw it back in my face," he added, screaming out the last part.

The torch bounced off her shoulder. Spots danced in her eyes and she felt her body crumbling. Pain-riddled and desperate, she tried to ward off the blows.

"Marty, no." Her pleas were ignored. He was past sense or reason.

This time when he hit her, the impact rocked her head to the side and the world bled out of focus. Barely aware of what she was doing, she rolled onto her stomach and clawed at the grass. Amidst the pain and shock, her brain took over and she moved on instinct. With her hair hanging over her face Beth made it half a metre before Marty landed the final blow.

Chapter Thirty

Marty moved with unhurried ease. Beth's lifeless body was heavier than he expected so placing her on the back seat took careful handling. Their life together was over, but he owed her gentleness even in death. Although the last few days had proved she was never really right for him, he still cared. He wasn't a monster.

She's beautiful. The paleness of her skin even with the bruises made her features appear like marble. She looked like a flawless sculpture in perfect repose. He brushed a strand of hair from her cheek and grimaced at the grit that clung to his fingers. He had idolised her and put her on too high a pedestal; he saw that now.

Outwardly, Beth had been perfection, but she lacked warmth. She never understood what he was working to achieve because Beth thought small. She was a small-minded woman. Worse, she held him back. He tucked her knees safely to the side then slammed the car door.

In a way, he was relieved that she had shown her true colours. It made saying goodbye easier. How could he have stayed knowing she had lied to him? Knowing she had tried to run away just when things got tough? Trying to sneak away when he needed her was the most unforgivable sin. You didn't turn on the person that fed and clothed you. His mother showed him that the hard way. Through painful but valuable lessons she taught him that loyalty was paramount.

Pike took some time and work and there was nothing gentle about the way Marty dragged his body from the cabin. The thud of Pike's boots on the steps sounded hollow, but the noise was quickly swallowed by the trees and the lake. The muffled bumping reminded Marty of the way Pike's feet had drummed in those last few seconds. When Marty drew the rope tighter, Pike had bucked and struggled and his legs had moved almost independently from his upper body. Strange.

By the time he reached the car, Marty was winded and his hands were slick with sweat. Dumping the body near the car, he went back inside and got a glass of water. There was no need to rush. Rushing led to mistakes and Marty had all night to do things right.

Leaning against the sink, he noticed Beth's suitcase. Her clothes were scattered and overflowing. He downed the water then tutted to himself before he got to work packing her things. She was careless with her belongings. There was never any thought for the cost and work that he put in so she could have designer clothes. But that was Beth: thoughtless, never once acknowledging that everything she owned was bought and paid for by the sweat off his back.

Her messiness should have been a red flag. Love is blind, he thought then sniffed one of her T-shirts. Her scent lingered, yet he was already thinking of her in the past tense. He had done the right thing. It would be hard for a while, but he'd been through worse. What was it his mother used to say?

"You'd miss a sore thumb if you had it long enough," he said then gathered up Beth's toiletries and tossed them in the suitcase.

His mother was a crazy bitch. He had the scars to prove it, but she had known how to put things in perspective.

He'd wasted time picking up after Beth, but living with her untidiness had been driving him nuts for so long, it felt nice to finally put things in order. Ever since they arrived at White Mist Lake, he longed for a clean slate – a blank page on which he could write a different story.

A clean page with a new story, or at least a new chapter. He had the money and finally there was quiet and order. Although what he would write hadn't come to him yet, and that *was* concerning. There was a foggy place burrowed amongst his plans where all he could see was that damn lake.

Back outside, he looked at Pike's body as it lay sprawled alongside the car's open boot. *You don't look like such a tough guy now*. Marty kicked Pike's head. It was going to be a bugger hauling Pike into the boot, but taking out the rubbish was never an easy job.

Half an hour later Marty was on his way with the shotgun propped on the floor in front of the passenger seat. Where did Beth get a shotgun? He made a mental note to have a look around when he got back to the retreat. Best to check and see if Beth's handyman friend was still hanging around.

Thoughts of Beth and the maintenance man were short lived as his mind returned to the shotgun. It was an old two-trigger unit, heavy and evil-looking. Driving with the shotgun as his companion made him feel like an old-time gunslinger. Shame he had to bury the thing with the rest of the stuff, but sentimentality could lead to slip-ups and he couldn't have that. He'd come too far and had done too much to have everything come undone because he'd kept a memento of his time at the lake.

The lake. The check-in woman and the deep movement of the water as her body went down, rushed back. How could it be so deep? Absently, he scratched at his wrist. He didn't want to think about the lake's depth and the way Tracy clawed at his hand as the weight of the rock pulled her under. He had thought she was dead until her hand reached up and then it was too late.

"It's done," he said and was almost surprised when Beth didn't answer from behind him. He had half-expected her to ask him what had been done.

"It's done and what's done can't be undone," he said and turned on the radio.

Pop music filled the cab, Beth's sort of music. He switched channels until he found soft jazz. The unpredictable beat soothed him. Beth's taste in music was atrocious. That alone should have given him pause, but he had overlooked it like he had so many of her other inadequacies. He'd learned a valuable lesson; he was grateful to Beth for that much.

* * *

The familiar landscape was welcoming even in the dark. This was his third visit. First, Hubbard, then back, not for the wedding ring – though finding it was good luck – but to bury the money.

The first time Pike texted him after the break-in, Marty had realised that keeping the money under the spare tyre in the boot was too dangerous.

"It's not over," Pike had texted.

Those three words had been enough to make going back to the burial site seem like a good idea. A risky move if Pike had been watching. He hadn't been, though. Marty was careful. He had kept too sharp of an eye on the roads and the retreat to be fooled. Still, it was better to put the money underground and out of harm's way. Not one hundred and fifty thousand as he'd told Beth, but closer to two hundred. His secret, just like the thirty thousand hidden under a false bottom in their bathroom cupboard.

"Sorry, pet," he said over his shoulder while keeping his gaze on the twisting trail that carved its way through the national park. "Some things are too good to share."

Glancing up, he was taken by the vastness of the night sky. A sudden desire to smell the air became almost as strong as his need to breathe. When he lowered the window, a breeze rushed in, wild and clean. The foggy area in his brain remained, but that was okay because it occupied the part of his mind that couldn't quite believe what he'd done to Beth – what he'd done to any of them.

* * *

Her arms flopped then rested against his back. She felt lighter this way, slung over his shoulder the same way he had once carried her into the river while she squealed with delight. The memory pushed in, but he forced his thoughts elsewhere – to Pike. He had taken Pike first, dragging and pulling and stopping to wipe the sweat from his brows. It took almost an hour to conquer the ten-minute walk then another forty minutes to dig the hole. The new grave was shallower than the first, but wider. Wide enough for two this time.

When he reached the clearing, he crouched and as he deposited Beth in the grave, he felt dampness on her pants. Her bladder had released and the wetness had seeped through her clothes. He shuddered with disgust then clambered out of the hole. Seeing Pike and Beth lying side by side like lovers, he forgot the urine and felt a stab of jealousy. She would be Pike's forever. There would be no more running away and no more secrets. The two of them now shared something more intimate than he and Beth ever had – death.

"You deserve each other," he said then laid the shotgun on top of Pike.

This was where it ended and there was relief in that knowledge. No more hiding his deepest thoughts. No more looking over his shoulder. He was a free man now.

Deep down he'd known it would have to be this way. He had known when he booked the cabin under the name David Freeman. He knew it would come to this, the moment Pike and Hubbard had broken into the house. He realised that once Beth learned the truth, she would become a problem. She would become a liability.

He stood and scrubbed his hands over his jeans and they came away damp and grimy. Something moved in the trees. It scuttled and shook the branches. An owl gave a lonely sounding hoot. The burial site was alive and dead at the same time. He thought the place comforting an hour ago, but now he wanted to be gone. The whispering leaves sounded too much like someone or something breathing. It made his skin prickle.

He glanced at the grave and for an instant he thought the faces had moved. Were they smiling? Fooling him? No, he told himself. It was only shadows thrown by the light of his torch. Still, he watched Beth's face and after a moment let out a nervous chuckle and turned away.

All that was left to do was to cover the bodies, unearth the money and then return to the retreat for a necessary clean-up. No time to get spooked. A decision had been made. When he got back, he wouldn't touch the woman in the lake. It was better she stayed in the water – better for the lake.

Chapter Thirty-one

The river rocked as her body bobbed on its gentle ebb. Blackness replaced the unmarred sky and Beth wondered why it was so dark, but it was only a momentary concern. She thought of the sandy shore that now seemed distant and unreachable. A blast of cold air suddenly touched her face and pain rushed in with piercing jabs of white-hot agony.

"Sorry, pet." Marty's voice came out of the dark.

Her lips moved soundlessly as music blared. The noise was an intrusion that vanished when nothingness engulfed her. No sooner than oblivion fell, she was again jolted with pain. This time her ribs twanged and her head was hot with a rush of blood. She felt fabric brush her cheek. She recognised the familiar scent of Marty's cologne; it mingled with other unpleasant smells on the night air.

The pain in her head was excruciating. It had a monstrous life of its own that eclipsed her will to struggle. It was only when she felt herself falling that the memories came back: Marty striking her, the torch in his hand as he closed in on her, and the recollection of terror and desperation. Memories of fear that tasted like metal in her mouth.

She opened her eyes and saw stars that blurred then settled. The perfect tiny dots of light reminded her that not only was she still alive, but that she was on her back and gazing up at the sky.

"You deserve each other."

Marty spoke, but the meaning behind his words seemed impossible to grasp.

Forcing her eyes to focus, she saw a beam of light. Something primal and raw inside her told her to stay still and wait for the light to move on. The beam disappeared and realisation hit. The earthy thick odour. The feel of dirt under her hands. A solid mass lying beside her. She was in a grave.

Blood roared in her ears and an urge to scream formed in her chest. She had every right to scream, but somehow she was able to suppress it.

The light returned and she snapped her eyes shut. Even through closed eyelids she could see the glare. Seconds went by – a long endless beat of holding her breath and willing her limbs to stay motionless. Finally, the light shifted and she allowed herself to breathe. Shallow breaths were all her aching ribs would allow.

Her left hand felt strangely numb so she used her right and touched the mass beside her. It was solid yet yielding. Her mind went to Lenton Hubbard. Was she in his grave and lying next to his decaying body? Her stomach cramped and she let out a whimper.

She clamped a hand over her mouth and gulped back the cries that rose into her throat. She needed to think, to block out the pain and horror, and act. If she didn't, she'd die. Maybe she was already close to death because every breath was a struggle and her mind longed for unconsciousness.

Using her right hand again, she grabbed hold of the thing beside her then pulled herself into a sitting position. As she moved to let go of it, her fingers brushed against cold metal. Instead of recoiling, she explored the object and was stunned at what she discovered. *The shotgun*. The stars told her that she was alive and the shotgun showed her she had a chance of staying that way.

She moved with the stiffness of an old woman as she struggled to rise further. Moving was painful, but the alternative of being buried alive was worse. Once she was sitting tall, she noticed other things. There was no foul odour of decay. That meant the body that occupied her grave was fresh. She prayed that Craig wasn't lying beside her, but with only a little moonlight and a faint glow from Marty's torch, she had no way of knowing.

There were seconds of silence and then the sliding and rustling of earth on metal. Marty was digging, but she had no time to ponder why. Nor did she have time to dwell on what he had done to her or the betrayal and savagery of his actions. That misery would come later if she lived through the night.

She grabbed the shotgun and pulled it into her lap, then felt for the grip and let her fingers explore it until she found the double trigger. Biting down as a flash of pain ripped through her, she used the shotgun as a crutch and found her footing. Finally, her head and shoulders were above ground and out of the grave.

The scene became clear and yet strangely off-kilter. She saw Marty. His back was to her as he crouched and clawed at the earth with a torch next to him. Not too far from her was a large rock bathed grey in the torchlight. Marty seemed too intent on whatever he was doing to hear her dragging herself out of the grave.

"Marty!" Her voice came out as a croak and the name barely whispered past her lips. "Marty!" she said with more force as she slid back the safety on the shotgun.

He froze.

With her legs unsteady, she lifted the shotgun with her right hand, but was only able to nudge the barrel up with her left.

Still crouched low, he turned. Despite the gloom, she saw shock on his face or perhaps that was what she had wanted to see. To him, she was a ghost and that was good because she wanted him to be scared.

"Thank God you're alive." His words dripped with insincerity. "I didn't mean to hurt you. Everything just got out of hand. I only wanted you to stop running. It was... It wasn't me," he stammered while keeping his eyes on the shotgun. "But you're alive. Thank God!"

"You already said that," she said while fighting to keep the shotgun level. "Give me the car keys." She spoke between short gasps.

He moved to stand and Beth used her left hand to bump the barrel to chest height. "Don't," she said.

"Okay, okay," he said and stayed down. "But I only want to help."

The torch next to him gave off enough light for them both to see – the same heavy metal cylinder torch. The one he used to bludgeon her. And maybe he *had* succeeded in his attempt to kill her because for a time she felt that she'd been far away from the lake and the burial site. She had been warm and safe, so peaceful and safe that she'd been reluctant to leave, but by choice or through the strength of her stubborn heart she was back. Now she was afraid, but also angry and determined to never again be his victim.

"You can't make it to the car in your condition," he said. "Let me help you. I can drive you to the hospital."

"Keys," she demanded while her vision blurred and she fought for every breath. "Now, Marty!"

"Beth, please just—"

"Put them on the rock and step away." She heard herself giving orders haltingly yet with clarity. Clarity was becoming hard to sustain. "Don't make me shoot you."

"You're not thinking straight. It's me," he implored.

"Yeah," she said. "I know exactly who you are. Now put the keys on the rock and get the fuck away."

Something in her voice got him moving. He shuffled sideways and pulled the car keys out of his pocket and after a second's hesitation he placed them on the rock.

"This is crazy. You don't have to do this alone. We decided to have a family, remember? Nothing's changed, pet." He was still talking, convinced he could charm and manipulate her into believing in him again. He was certain that if he stabbed at her weak spot she'd fall for his lies. And why not? It had always worked in the past.

"Leave the torch and get over there," she said jerking her chin toward the grave she had crawled out of.

He rose with his hands held up and still speaking in that ever so reasonable voice, he moved toward the grave. "I love you, Beth. We can go away together."

"Now get in," she instructed. "Get in and lie down."

"Please, pet. You don't look good. You need help."

She knew he was stalling.

"Get in!" Her voice was shrill, almost a scream, but she didn't care. There was no one to disturb but the dead and she was running out of time.

Her body was weakening and the shotgun felt like an impossible weight. Keeping her strangely narrow gaze on Marty was vital because her strength was apt to fail at any moment.

Marty was at the grave. There were only a few metres between him, the rock, and her.

"Do it," she said, motioning for him to get into the hole.

He bent and she felt a small sliver of relief. It was then she realised that he wasn't stooping to jump into the grave, but to grab the spade. Why hadn't she seen the spade?

Marty moved with lightning speed, snatching up the spade and crossing the short distance between them. Without hesitation he swung. Somehow, Beth managed to sidestep, but her movement gave her only a fraction of a second before he was able to close in.

More out of panic than intention, she pulled the trigger and the shotgun roared. The kickback jolted her upper body and she fell back as fire raced over her ribs. There was silence and then what sounded like an updraft of air as her eardrums vibrated from the blast.

Kilometres of the sky came into view, and she realised she was on her back again. The first real noise she was aware of was groaning. Clutching her side to minimise the pain, she struggled onto her feet.

Marty lay sprawled against the rock. It was too dark to tell if he'd been shot. Her first instinct was to go to him and check if he was injured, but her old instincts were the enemy now.

With painful deliberateness she picked up the shotgun and circled him. When she was behind his head and at a safe distance, she retrieved the torch. Its barrel had a greasy feel that made her grimace.

She directed the beam to the rock and saw that its jagged edge was coated with blood. Marty lay with his head turned to the side, only centimetres from the bloody rock. She shone the light over his face and saw that his eyes were closed, but his mouth was moving, emitting gurgling groans.

Instead of reaching to help him, she grabbed the car keys and stuffed them in her pocket. With the torch clamped under her left arm and the shotgun in her right, she turned to flee then stopped. No matter how much she wanted to run, she had to know. She had to be sure.

Limping, she went back to the grave and set the shotgun down. Until then she had only been aware of the cold as a secondary symptom, but now her damp and dirt-covered clothes hung from her skin like an icy shell, making her shudder so hard that the torchlight jerked from tree to tree. The old growth of the forest jumped at her. Tree trunks, like spectral faces, were bathed grey-blue in the skipping light and branches seemed to lean in and surround her.

"Please, please, please," she whispered then shone the light into the hole.

She saw scuffed black boots and black jeans. Was Craig wearing black jeans? Her mind was blank of all things except the biting cold and the creeping feeling that something was about to grab her and thrust her into the grave.

When the beam landed on the face, she let out a strangled cry. It was Pike and not Craig. Her relief was quickly eaten by revulsion, not because of the body, but what had been done to Pike. His eyes were open, but the orbs were red with blood. His tongue protruded from his lips like a thick blue slug. More blood covered his lips and trailed from the corners of his mouth, giving him a vampiric look.

She stepped back, desperate to get away from the ghastly corpse, when the ground collapsed and she found herself falling. With the damp earth shifting beneath her, she clawed at the air. This time she did scream: a piercing primal howl that seemed to fill her entire skull. It was a scream that heralded madness. Beth knew if she fell onto the dead thing and inhaled its gassy scent, it would send her over the edge and into insanity.

She was still screaming when her butt hit the edge of the hole. The collapsed dirt scuttled into the grave. Her leg was dangling only centimetres above the body, but she was okay and still above ground. This time she ran. Leaving the shotgun behind, she gripped the torch terrified at the thought of being in the dark with the dead.

Chapter Thirty-two

It was minutes before she had any sense of which way she was going or how fast she'd been moving. The torch slipped from her hand twice, before she realised she had to slow down or she risked falling. If she went down, she feared she might never get up.

Moving in little more than a lurching walk, her pace became torturously slow. Every snapped twig startled and terrified her. With each sound she imagined Marty circling her and chasing her like an animal. Every branch that brushed her cheek was Pike's dead fingers dragging her back to the grave to lie with him.

Finally, she stumbled to a stop. Confused, she turned around only to see that all directions appeared identical. It was impossible to judge how far she had come. The track and the car might be a few metres ahead or kilometres in the other direction.

Blind panic had driven her and now her body was exhausted. If she didn't stop and take things in, she might blunder around until her legs gave out. But she was so cold – colder than she'd ever been before. Her fingers were cramping and her eyelids were as heavy as lead. Sleep beckoned. A few minutes curled into a ball or resting her head against a tree trunk would be enough. Maybe if she closed her eyes, it would be easier to think.

Don't fall asleep when you're cold and exhausted. Wasn't that what they said? She had no idea who 'they' were, but she did remember hearing the advice, so instead of giving in she stumbled on. With each slogging step, she believed that the advice to keep moving was something given by people who had never known what it was like to be this weary. So weary that contemplating climbing over a fallen log seemed like standing at the foot of a mountain – a mountain where a flag fluttered triumphantly in the breeze.

She blinked and realised that what she was looking at wasn't a flag, but a strip of the silky blue pyjama fabric. The same fabric she had torn and wrapped around her hat. Looking at the material was like gazing into a dark tunnel that led years into the past – a past too distant to have taken place only a few days ago.

Despite the pain and terror, she let out a laugh. They'd been so careful that night, so determined not to leave any trace of their presence behind for fear it would be their undoing. Yet here it was, and it wasn't their undoing but her last hope for survival. The bit of cloth was a sign that she was heading in the right direction; a burst of hope to keep her going.

A branch crackled, its sound as brittle and sharp as gunfire in a silent forest. An animal or Marty? She got moving. She didn't trust herself to climb over the fallen log. Instead, she rolled over it head first and on her stomach. Things were coming back to her now. She and Marty had dragged Lenton's body over the same log after they'd been walking for ten minutes and had made little progress. If she picked up her pace, the car should be about forty metres ahead.

As she moved, she heard more noises: rustling and repetitive crunching. Not the sounds that kangaroos made. An emu perhaps, but she was sure the giant birds slept at night. When she paused, the sounds ceased, only to begin again when she moved. The further she went the more certain she was that Marty was following. A few more steps and she lost control and put on a burst of speed.

Running, or as close to it as she could manage, she broke from between the trees and finally hit the trail, laughing like a mad woman. Just the feel of the packed dirt under her feet was enough to turn her laughter into tears, but she laughed again when she spotted the Mazda. Like a moonlit mirage, it was parked within an arm's length.

Her moment of elation was short lived and quickly overtaken by panic. Marty was close. She also believed that if she hesitated, like a mirage, the car would waver out of existence. An irrational fear, but one powerful enough to make her reach out and touch the Mazda's bumper. The solid feel of the cold plastic was reassuring, but time was wasting.

Remembering the keys, she ripped them from her pocket and pressed the unlock button. A few seconds later she sat behind the wheel breathing in the faint scent of Marty's cologne. Glancing towards the trees, she saw no sign of him, but as she looked away, she was sure she caught movement out of the corner of her eye.

With her hands trembling, she locked the doors and threw the car into gear. When she stepped on the accelerator, nothing happened. It took a frenzied second for her to realise that the car was in neutral and the handbrake was on.

"Stupid," she muttered then shifted gears and turned on the headlights.

When she looked up, Marty was on the track. In the glare of the lights, he shouldered the shotgun and aimed it at her. Her heart gave a series of irregular beats.

"Beth!" he screamed in a voice she barely recognised.

She knew he would never let her go, not while he was alive. He'd follow her wherever she went. Absurdly, the words *couples therapy* jumped into her mind. With her hands clenched on the steering wheel and her arms locked ramrod straight, she floored the accelerator.

The car raced forward. Dirt and stones sprayed the sides of the car as it closed in on Marty. Instead of firing, he dove left. There was no crunch or impact, but that didn't mean she had missed him entirely. Alive or dead, she left him behind. There was no time to look back.

* * *

Sometime later, the tyres hit solid road. Beth had no idea where she was, but she was alive and out of the national park. She knew she wasn't leaving by the same entrance they had used. This road looked similar in appearance, but she guessed she was on the other side of the reserve.

There were no streetlights on these country roads and the absolute darkness made it feel like civilisation was a faraway memory. She flicked on the high beam and then the heater. Warm air flooded the cab and with it her arms and hands relaxed. It would take some time before the shivers eased.

She drove for what seemed like an hour with the headlights as the only illumination for as far as her blurred vision could see. Without warning a car sped by, its back draft rocking the Mazda.

She braked and hit the horn, willing the other car to stop. In the rear-view mirror she watched taillights disappear without slowing. It was a good sign, she told herself as she continued on. Another car meant more populated roads, the kind of roads that led to houses and service stations. Realisation suddenly hit. She'd forgotten about the navigation system.

"Yes!" she almost shouted.

Slowing down, she scanned the complicated series of buttons and controls that framed the small screen on the dashboard. Marty, ever cautious about their movements being tracked, had turned the system off a few days ago.

Trust him to know every control and function in the damn car, she thought with something that felt like hatred – only deeper and impossible to articulate. She wished she'd hit him with the car. She gritted her teeth. Then he would know what it was like to be brutalised by the person who was supposed to love you above all others.

The taste of vengeance became as sweet as oranges on her lips. A piercing jab of agony stabbed at her ribs and she was horrified to realise that she had blacked out for a few seconds and the car had slowed to the point of rolling.

I'm losing it. She wouldn't be able to function for much longer. Focusing on the dashboard required every scrap of her concentration, so she hit the brake. The first button she pressed caused the hazard lights to flash and then she pressed another and, unexpectedly, the small screen came to life.

A map appeared telling her she was on Angelson Drive. The name gave her pause. She wasn't superstitious, but she wanted to believe the road name was a good omen. God knew she was due for one.

After the system was operational, she drew a blank. An address. A destination. She needed to reach somewhere there would be a phone. The only thing she could come up with was Bunbury so she typed in the name. The device took a second then spat out directions. She couldn't quite muster enough strength to laugh, but she smiled. Illuminated by the brightly coloured screen, her expression looked more like a pained grimace.

Soon the road widened. White lines appeared and were quickly followed by distant lights. She was still twenty-five kilometres from her destination when she saw a sign for a deer park. A minute later she drove onto the turn-off.

When she reached the park, there was eerie silence. The headlights picked out darkened stables and then a small herd of deer. The animals' eyes turned into red pupilless stones and they regarded the car with wariness. Finally, she saw lights.

She rolled to a stop and leaned on the horn. When her hand lost strength, she let her head rest on the steering wheel and fancied she heard voices. Doors opened. Lifting her head was a gargantuan effort, but when she did, there was a face at the window. She unlocked the door and a stranger pulled it open.

"White Mist Lake. Ambulance," she stammered then leaned back and allowed her eyes to close.

Chapter Thirty-three

There was too much movement and confusion. She tried to ask about Craig, but her questions were ignored amid the rush of activity. She was strapped to a board with an oxygen mask clamped over her face. The same questions were asked over and over.

"What's your name? Were you attacked? Do you know where you are?"

Talking had become difficult so she was at the mercy of strangers. For some reason the paramedics answered her questions with questions. No one seemed to be listening to what was most important, to what she was trying to say.

The door of the ambulance closed and it felt like she was floating. Pain was constant, but at times felt distant. She was no longer being hunted and, although breathing hurt, each breath felt lighter. There was still fear, but now it was of what was to come and not who was coming after her.

In the blink of an eye, she was out of the ambulance and hurtling through corridors. Strange faces. More questions. Frightening words bounced back and forth: fracture, next of kin, surgery. The words made sense yet meant nothing.

* * *

"Will you stay?" Beth asked.

Since her second surgery, she had become child-like and helpless and wanted nothing more than her mother's stoic presence.

"Are you sure you're ready?" her mother asked.

They were in Royal Perth Hospital, hundreds of kilometres from White Mist Lake. Beth had eventually reached Bunbury, but not under her own steam. Her memory of events after being taken into the ambulance was a cloudy puddle. The surface was deceptively clear, but her thoughts kept going back to dirt, flashes of light, and dark water.

All she knew was what she'd been told. Her injuries had required more than could be managed at a country hospital. A dislocated shoulder, three broken ribs, and surgery to repair an orbital fracture. Her eye socket, she later learned, had been badly injured and emergency surgery had been necessary to repair the damage and minimise further harm to the optic nerve. A few hours later she had been rushed back into theatre to remove a clot that had formed in her right lung.

Days of pain meds followed and her body became the property of others: a thing to be monitored, observed, and bathed. Every waking moment was spent suffering or in dread of where it would all end. Above all things, she recalled the dread. In some ways those cold and half-remembered hours were worse than her injuries. Perhaps not worse but a close second, she decided as she held a mirror up to examine her distorted features.

She stowed the mirror on the locker beside the bed as her mother went out to speak to two police officers that were waiting in the corridor. The detectives had been turned away once by her doctor, but now Beth was determined to take the first step toward ending the nightmare.

After greeting the detectives, she felt self-conscious because of the swelling on her face and the thick, unfamiliar sound of her voice. Her physical injuries made her feel diminished and guilty as though the bruises and bandages were evidence of her part in the crimes committed at White Mist Lake.

The officers introduced themselves: a woman named Lowery and a younger man named Balacci. Nothing was said, but Beth had the impression that the woman was in charge.

"Mrs Jacobsen," Detective Lowery began as she seated herself next to the bed.

She had sombre eyes and calm hands that relaxed in her lap while the other detective, Balacci, produced a notebook and pen. As Balacci stood poised to write, the dread that had been coiled in Beth's gut tightened. She had rehearsed the words in her mind a dozen times, but the weight of Lowery's gaze reminded her of the dark waters of the lake and suddenly her tongue was as dry as a dusty rag.

"You told the paramedics that your husband attacked you," Lowery began.

At the mention of Marty, Beth couldn't help but glance at her mother. They hadn't discussed what had happened, but all of the unasked questions were there in her mother's apprehensive look and stiff posture. Talking about the night that Marty almost beat her to death felt like a knife in an already open wound *and* an assault on both mother and daughter. Beth wanted to recoil from the guilt and humiliation. She craved a drink to blur the edges and moisten her lips. Just a few sips to work their magic in a way that pain medication could never deliver.

The detectives were watching and weighing her reactions. Beth could almost see herself through Lowery's eyes: a pathetic woman, a battered wife, a person who had committed crimes for the man who brutalised her, a woman with no job, no money, and no ambition beyond an easy, pampered life. A stupid woman who thought a few slaps now and then were acceptable because her husband always bought her something nice afterwards. Because he always said sorry.

Beth saw all these things all too clearly, but what she couldn't quite understand was how she had let it go so far.

"But that doesn't explain what we found at White Mist Lake. Can you fill in the blanks and help us get a clear picture of how you came to be at the deer park on the night of the twenty-fourth?" Lowery pressed. "The retreat owner, Mr Williams, said a man attacked him in the office. He said you tried to help him."

It took Beth a beat to absorb the words. The detective was talking about Craig. She had spent days in a cocoon of sedation, asking for information, but up until now none had been forthcoming. Braced for the worst, she wasn't prepared for the relief that came with knowing that Craig was alive and not another name to be added to the list of destruction that she and Marty had visited on everyone they touched.

"Craig's alive?" Beth asked.

Lowery answered with more questions. "Mrs Jacobsen, did your husband try to kill Craig Williams? Do you know anything about Tracy Williams? She's been missing for six days."

Beth touched a hand to her swollen face. "Yes. I know where Tracy is."

The story came out slowly. The two detectives listened. At one point Lowery stopped and gave Beth a formal caution; some spiel about not having to say anything, but Beth simply agreed and pushed on. Balacci took notes and Lowery asked her to repeat parts and to clarify events and timelines. At one point Beth's mother took her hand while Beth sipped from a glass of water. Beth told them everything, every raw detail and while she knew she was incriminating herself, there was relief in knowing it was finally over. Whatever happened now would be better than holding the ghastly secrets inside.

After almost two hours, Paulette said, "I think that's enough. My daughter's exhausted and needs to rest."

"All right," Detective Lowery said giving Paulette a tight smile. "We'll verify the information she's given us." She looked at Beth. "You're not under arrest at this time, but I have to warn you that if all this pans out, you may be facing serious charges. And there's still the question of your—"

Beth nodded, but Paulette stood and cut Lowery off. "Yes, we realise that *and* my daughter has been extremely cooperative. Next time you speak to her, she will have a solicitor present."

Detective Lowery's sombre gaze focused intently on Paulette Rowe. "Yes," she replied before leaving. "That might be a good idea."

"Wait," Beth said then sat forward and winced at the pain in her shoulder. "What about Marty?"

For the first time since she had entered the room, Detective Lowery appeared at a loss. "We have no idea where your husband is, Mrs Jacobsen."

Chapter Thirty-four

The house was no longer a crime scene, but the reminders of the forensic team's work were everywhere. The kitchen was coated in black dust, drawers hung open, and the floor was marked with tape and littered with scraps of paper packaging. The new window was covered with smudge marks. The bedroom was in a similar state only with shards of glass still covering the bed.

The prospect of cleaning the house with only one arm was so overwhelming that Beth wasn't surprised when tears welled. If she gave in to them, the tears would turn into a crying fit, and she had endured enough meltdowns to last a lifetime. Besides, her eye throbbed and the last thing she needed was to have to blot at her swollen face with tissue paper.

She walked from room to room trying to summon the strength to start cleaning. For now, the house was still her home and the only one she had. Sobbing wouldn't change the fact that there was work to be done and not just on setting the house to rights but also on herself.

It had been seven days since her last drink – seven long days. Five nights in hospital and three in a motel room that she had shared with her mother. Two of those nights were spent waiting for the police to allow her back into her own house and then another night waiting for the new window to be installed to replace the one Angel had leapt through. Despite everything that had happened she had longed for these familiar walls.

Still wandering, she found herself back in the kitchen and staring at the dog door. Angel's door. A reminder of his absence. How long had Angel been boarded? More than ten days. Time had slipped away in a maelstrom of violence and drama. Amidst everything she'd been through, Angel had been waiting. Now she could bring him home. It was the one thing she *could* fix.

Marty's Mazda had been impounded, but her keys were on the counter and her car was still in the driveway. What was to stop her from picking up Angel first thing in the morning? She could make it with one hand. She'd certainly driven under worse circumstances. The idea sparked a flicker of enthusiasm. It had been so long since she experienced the emotion that it took her by surprise.

Angel's presence would reanimate the house. His gentle eyes and steadfast love would heal her. They would heal each other. It was funny, she thought. If not for Marty, she would have never had Angel in the first place. Maybe something good had come out of the marriage.

"Thanks, asshole," she said to the empty house.

Another idea occurred to her – a divorce. Why not find a solicitor and start the process? *I'll need a team of solicitors at this rate.* For the first time in a long while, she smiled without a trace of bitterness or acrimony.

Her to-do list was growing. Pick up Angel and divorce Marty. Surely, attempted murder was grounds for a divorce. Beth wasn't sure if a person still needed grounds to get a divorce, but if it *was* still a requirement, she was sure her predicament would fit the bill. It felt good to have a plan; a clear objective. She was starting to understand why Marty loved plans. He'll be my ex-husband soon, she thought and braced herself for a torrent of emotion, but there was only relief and the embers of sadness.

With the decision made she opened the cupboard and pulled out a can of bug spray. She doubted there was a living insect within a twenty-metre radius thanks to Marty's loathing of bugs. She set the can on the counter so she could reach a roll of large, black garbage bags. Once she had what she needed, she headed toward the bedroom.

She had promised the doctors and her mother that she would rest, but breaking promises was her new way of life. Stripping the bed with one arm was tricky, but she managed. Scooping the glass up with the bedding, she dumped everything in the bag then used the stick vacuum to clean the carpet.

Fatigued but determined to keep the momentum going, she fetched clean sheets from the laundry. Plain white cotton sheets replaced the red silky ones that had been stuffed into the garbage bag and dumped in the hall. By the time the room was in order she was sweating, exhausted, and half-wishing she hadn't been so quick to insist that her mother return to Albany.

It wasn't just fatigue that weighed her down, but ghosts. The house was crowded with them, but if she was serious about changing her life, she'd have to face them alone. The temptation to lean on her mother was strong, but Beth had been reliant on emotional and liquid crutches for far too long. Besides, she needed time to think and lick her wounds. Time to begin reclaiming herself and she needed to do that under her own steam.

Done with the room, she stared at the neatly made bed with its hospital corners and tight tucks. She could almost hear Marty's voice. *If the corners aren't tucked, the bed's only half made.* She tutted then yanked the sheets lose. A small victory, but it was a start. Old habits were breaking and it felt good.

* * *

The sun was going down and the idea of being in the dark turned her thoughts to White Mist Lake and to graves and clearings that were hidden deep in the forest. As she returned to the kitchen, she turned on every light. On the way through, she flicked on the TV hoping the chatter would drive away the chill that was creeping over her bones. As tragic as it was, she wanted to believe that her body was just craving alcohol, but it was more than that. It was the house and the memories and the trauma. It was the knowledge that Marty was still out there.

He wouldn't come back. The police were sure he was on the run or dead somewhere in the forest. It would be insane for him to come within kilometres of the house. The cops were watching and driving by every hour. They assured her there was nothing to fear. But they didn't know Marty.

Satisfied that she had done enough for one night, she flopped on the sofa and stared at the TV. Instead of a mind-numbing reality show, an image of White Mist Lake appeared on the screen and all her plans and resolutions evaporated.

> *This tranquil setting has been the home of numerous grizzly crimes. The former owner of the retreat, Glen Williams, murdered his wife then took his own life. Now, the property is back in the headlines. Police have revealed that the current owner, Tracy Williams, the daughter of the previous owners, has been murdered and a section of Benchley Lyon's Reserve is now the focus of a search. It's still unclear what the police are hoping to find in the national park, but for now the usually quiet reserve is the scene of a massive search.*

It took time for the reporter's spiel to sink in and for Beth to realise she wasn't losing her mind. The retreat wasn't appearing on her screen like a misty spectre. What she was seeing was a news report. It shouldn't have been a surprise that the story had made the headlines, yet somehow seeing it on TV shook her to the core. Her crimes were now public knowledge and soon her name would be added to the reports. What's more, if the reporter was correct, Craig's father had murdered his wife at the lake.

I like it not. The words came back and goosebumps skipped over her arms. She didn't believe in real ghosts, but that place was hard to look at even on television. In her mind, she could still see the water, dark and bottomless, and the mist rolling off the lake like an exhaled breath.

She clicked off the TV and dropped the remote on the couch. Craig had suffered so much tragedy and she had added to it. He lost his sister to the lake because she and Marty brought their misery into Tracy and Craig's already scarred lives. The things Craig told her about Tracy, about her often needing to get away from the retreat and how he didn't like staying at the place if he didn't have to, all made more sense now. All those people lost to the lake.

Lost to the lake. She couldn't rationalise why she saw it that way, yet it was true. The knowledge was not her mind's way of shifting guilt. She was guilty and would always carry that burden. But the lake had its own energy – a dark vigour that welcomed violence. It whispered to the violent mind. She knew this in a flat, unshakable way. She knew because she had heard its call. Perhaps not with the same strength as some, but it whispered nonetheless. It whispered and it waited for a willing ear.

The path her thoughts had taken made her shiver. There was wine in the fridge. A glass would soften the edges and blur the memories. A couple of glasses and she would have a dreamless night's sleep instead of one where she was plagued by Tracy's bloated face. She went to the kitchen and pulled out the bottle. She stood over the sink holding the wine, her mouth shamefully watering.

Finally, she upended the bottle and let its contents trickle down the drain. She had won tonight's battle, but there would be more nights. More battles. For now, it was enough. It was early, only a little after seven o'clock, but she was both physically and emotionally spent. It was time for a hot shower and an early night.

Chapter Thirty-five

She hesitated. Dressed in fleecy pants and a loose top, she paused with her hand on the bathroom doorknob. Rather than soothe her nerves, the long shower had set her mind on a new track, one filled with nagging doubt. Something was off in the house. She had missed something vital, but what that something was wouldn't come to her. It circled her thoughts and danced just out of reach. The more she tried to grasp it the more slippery the information became.

"Just exhaustion," she said and opened the door.

While standing in the hallway, she listened. Silence. With near obsessive deliberateness, she went over the steps she had taken before her shower. Every door was locked and every window closed. There was no way in. Marty was long gone and even if he did try to return, she had his keys.

"There's no way in," she mumbled and padded into the bedroom.

Her phone rang from the kitchen and she gasped at the suddenness of its trill. It would be her mother calling the cheap mobile that Beth had bought at the supermarket. Her old phone had been left behind at the retreat or taken by Marty. If it still had been at the lake when the police

Also by Anna Willett

BACKWOODS RIPPER
RETRIBUTION RIDGE
UNWELCOME GUESTS
FORGOTTEN CRIMES
CRUELTY'S DAUGHTER
VENGEANCE BLIND
THE WOMAN BEHIND HER
DEAR NEIGHBOUR
THE FAMILY MAN

SMALL TOWN NIGHTMARE
COLD VALLEY NIGHTMARE
SAVAGE BAY NIGHTMARE

PEST
BEAST

FREE with Kindle Unlimited and available in paperback from Amazon.

Printed in Dunstable, United Kingdom

65271905R00133